THE QUEEN
OF THE SWORDS

CORUM BOOK 2

A
GIFT TO THE
GLOUCESTER LIBRARY
FROM THE
J. EDWIN TREAKLE
FOUNDATION, INC

Also available from Michael Moorcock, Titan Books and Titan Comics

A NOMAD OF THE TIME STREAMS

The Warlord of the Air

The Land Leviathan

The Steel Tsar

THE ETERNAL CHAMPION SERIES

The Eternal Champion

Phoenix in Obsidian

The Dragon in the Sword

THE CORUM SERIES

The Knight of the Swords

The King of the Swords (July 2015)

The Bull and the Spear (August 2015)

The Oak and the Ram (September 2015)

The Sword and the Stallion (October 2015)

THE CORNELIUS QUARTET

The Final Programme (February 2016)

A Cure for Cancer (March 2016)

The English Assassin (April 2016)

The Condition of Muzak (May 2016)

THE MICHAEL MOORCOCK LIBRARY

Elric of Melniboné

Elric: Sailor on the Seas of Fate

MICHAEL MOORCOCK'S ELRIC

Volume 1: The Ruby Throne

Volume 2: Stormbringer

MICHAEL MOORCOCK

THE QUEEN OF THE SWORDS

CORUM BOOK 2

Gloucester Library
P.O. Box 2380
Gloucester, VA 23061

TITAN BOOKS

The Queen of the Swords
Print edition ISBN: 9781783291670
E-book edition ISBN: 9781783291663

Published by Titan Books
A division of Titan Publishing Group Ltd
144 Southwark Street, London SE1 0UP

First Titan edition: June 2015
12345678910

This is a work of fiction. Names, characters, places, and incidents either are the product of the author's imagination or are used fictitiously, and any resemblance to actual persons, living or dead, business establishments, events, or locales is entirely coincidental. The publisher does not have any control over and does not assume any responsibility for author or third-party websites or their content.

Copyright © 1971, 2015 by Michael Moorcock. All rights reserved.

Edited by John Davey

No part of this publication may be reproduced, stored in a retrieval system, or transmitted, in any form or by any means without the prior written permission of the publisher, nor be otherwise circulated in any form of binding or cover other than that in which it is published and without a similar condition being imposed on the subsequent purchaser.

A CIP catalogue record for this title is available from the British Library.

Printed and bound in the United States

Did you enjoy this book? We love to hear from our readers.
Please email us at: readerfeedback@titanemail.com or write to us at
Reader Feedback at the above address.

To receive advance information, news, competitions, and exclusive offers online, please sign up for the Titan newsletter on our website: www.titanbooks.com

This book is for Diane Boardman

 INTRODUCTION

I N THOSE DAYS there were oceans of light and cities in the skies and wild flying beasts of bronze. There were herds of crimson cattle that roared and were taller than castles. There were shrill, viridian things that haunted bleak rivers. It was a time of gods, manifesting themselves upon our world in all her aspects; a time of giants who walked on water; of mindless sprites and misshapen creatures who could be summoned by an ill-considered thought but driven away only on pain of some fearful sacrifice; of magics, phantasms, unstable nature, impossible events, insane paradoxes, dreams come true, dreams gone awry, of nightmares assuming reality.

It was a rich time and a dark time. The time of the Sword Rulers. The time when the Vadhagh and the Nhadragh, age-old enemies, were dying. The time when Man, the slave of fear, was emerging, unaware that much of the terror he experienced was the result of nothing else but the fact that he, himself, had come into existence. It was one of many ironies connected with Man (who, in those days, called his race "Mabden").

The Mabden lived brief lives and bred prodigiously. Within a few centuries they rose to dominate the westerly continent on which they had evolved. Superstition stopped them from sending many of their ships towards Vadhagh and Nhadragh lands for another century or two, but gradually they gained courage when no resistance was offered. They began to feel jealous of the older races; they began to feel malicious.

The Vadhagh and the Nhadragh were not aware of this. They had dwelt a million or more years upon the planet which now, at last, seemed at rest. They knew of the Mabden but considered them not greatly different from other beasts. Though continuing to indulge their traditional hatreds of one another, the Vadhagh and the Nhadragh spent their long hours in considering abstractions, in the creation of works of art and the like. Rational, sophisticated, at one with themselves, these older races were unable to believe in the changes that had come. Thus, as it almost always is, they ignored the signs.

There was no exchange of knowledge between the two ancient enemies, even though they had fought their last battle many centuries before.

The Vadhagh lived in family groups occupying isolated castles scattered across a continent called by them Bro-an-Vadhagh. There was scarcely any communication between these families, for the Vadhagh had long since lost the impulse to travel. The Nhadragh lived in their cities built on the islands in the seas to the north-west of Bro-an-Vadhagh. They, also, had little contact, even with their closest kin. Both races reckoned themselves invulnerable. Both were wrong.

Upstart Man was beginning to breed and spread like a pestilence across the world. This pestilence struck down the Old

Races wherever it touched them. And it was not only death that Man brought, but terror, too. Willfully, he made of the older world nothing but ruins and bones. Unwittingly, he brought psychic and supernatural disruption of a magnitude which even the Great Old Gods failed to comprehend.

And the Great Old Gods began to know Fear.

And Man, slave of fear, arrogant in his ignorance, continued his stumbling progress. He was blind to the huge disruptions aroused by his apparently petty ambitions. As well, Man was deficient in sensitivity, had no awareness of the multitude of dimensions that filled the universe, each plane intersecting with several others. Not so the Vadhagh or the Nhadragh, who had known what it was to move at will between the dimensions they termed the Five Planes. They had glimpsed and understood the nature of the many planes, other than the Five, through which the Earth moved.

Therefore it seemed a dreadful injustice that these wise races should perish at the hands of creatures who were still little more than animals. It was as if vultures feasted on and squabbled over the paralyzed body of the youthful poet who could only stare at them with puzzled eyes as they slowly robbed him of an exquisite existence they would never appreciate, never know they were taking.

"If they valued what they stole, if they knew what they were destroying," says the old Vadhagh in the story, *Now The Clouds Have Meaning*, "then I would be consoled."

It was unjust.

By creating Man, the universe had betrayed the Old Races.

But it was a perpetual and familiar injustice. The sentient may perceive and love the universe, but the universe cannot perceive and love the sentient. The universe sees no distinction between the multitude of creatures and elements which comprise it. All are equal. None is favoured. The universe, equipped with nothing but the materials and the power of creation, continues to create: something of this, something of that. It cannot control what it creates and it cannot, it seems, be controlled by its creations (though a few might deceive themselves otherwise). Those who curse the workings of the universe curse that which is deaf. Those who strike out at those workings fight that which is inviolate. Those who shake their fists, shake their fists at blind stars.

But this does not mean that there are some who will not try to do battle with and destroy the invulnerable.

There will always be such beings, sometimes beings of great wisdom, who cannot bear to believe in an insouciant universe.

Prince Corum Jhaelen Irsei was one of these. Perhaps the last of the Vadhagh race, he was sometimes known as the Prince in the Scarlet Robe.

This chronicle concerns him.

We have already learned how the Mabden followers of Earl Glandyth-a-Krae (who called themselves the Denledhyssi—or murderers) killed Prince Corum's relatives and his nearest kin and thus taught the Prince in the Scarlet Robe how to hate, how to kill and how to desire vengeance. We have heard how Glandyth tortured Corum and took away a hand and an eye and how Corum was rescued by the Giant of Laahr and taken to the castle of the Margravine Rhalina—a castle set upon a mount surrounded by the sea. Though Rhalina was a Mabden woman (of the gentler folk of Lywm-an-Esh) Corum and she fell in love. When Glandyth roused the Pony Tribes, the forest barbarians, to attack the Margravine's castle, she and Corum sought supernatural aid and thus fell into the hands of the sorcerer Shool, whose domain was the island called Svi-an-Fanla-Brool—Home of the Gorged God. And now Corum had direct experience of the morbid, unfamiliar powers at work in the world. Shool spoke of dreams and realities. ("I see you are beginning to argue in Mabden terms," he told Corum. "It is just as well for you, if you wish to survive in this Mabden dream." – "It is a dream…?" said Corum. – "Of sorts. Real enough. It is what you might call the dream of a god. There again you might say that it is a dream that a god has allowed to become reality. I refer of course to the Knight of the Swords who rules the Five Planes.")

With Rhalina his prisoner Shool could make a bargain with Corum. He gave him two gifts—the Hand of Kwll and the Eye of Rhynn—to replace his own missing organs. These jeweled and alien things were once the property of two brother gods known as the Lost Gods since they mysteriously vanished.

Now Shool told Corum what he must do if he wished to see Rhalina saved. Corum must go to the Realm of the Knight of the Swords—Lord Arioch of Chaos who ruled the Five Planes since he had wrested them from the control of Lord Arkyn of Law. There Corum must find the heart of the Knight of the Swords—a thing which was kept in a tower of his castle and which enabled him to take material shape on Earth and thus wield power (without a material shape—or a number of them—the Lords of Chaos could not rule mortals).

With little hope, Corum set off in a boat for the domain of Arioch but on his way was wrecked when a huge giant passed by him, merely fishing. In the land of the strange Ragha-da-Kheta he discovered that the eye could summon dreadful beings from those worlds to aid him—also the hand seemed to sense danger before it came and was ruthless in slaying even when Corum did not desire to slay. Then he realized that, by accepting Shool's gifts, he had accepted the logic of Shool's world and could not escape from it now.

During these adventures Corum learned of the eternal struggle between Law and Chaos. A cheerful traveler from Lywm-an-Esh enlightened him. It was, he said, "the Chaos Lords' will that rules you. Arioch is one of them. Long since there was a war between the forces of Order and the forces of Chaos. The forces of Chaos won and came to dominate the Fifteen Planes and, as I understand it, much that lies beyond them. Some say that Order was defeated completely and all her gods vanished. They say the Cosmic Balance tipped too far in one direction and that is why there are so many arbitrary events taking place in the world. They say that once the world was round instead of dish-shaped…" – "Some Vadhagh legends say it was once round," Corum informed him. – "Aye. Well, the Vadhagh began their rise before Order was banished. That is why the Sword Rulers hate the Old Races so much. They are not their creation at all. But the Great Gods are not allowed to interfere too directly in mortal affairs, so they have worked through the Mabden, chiefly…" – Corum, said: "Is this the truth?" – Hanafax shrugged. "It is *a* truth."

Later, in the Flamelands where the Blind Queen Ooresé lived, Corum saw a mysterious figure who almost immediately vanished after he had slain poor Hanafax with the Hand of Kwll (which knew Hanafax would betray him). He learned that Arioch was the Knight of the Swords and that Xiombarg was the Queen of the Swords ruling the next group of Five Planes, while the most powerful Sword Ruler of all ruled the last of the Five Planes— Mabelode, King of the Swords. Corum learned that all the hearts of the Sword Rulers were hidden where even they could not touch them. But after further adventures in Arioch's castle, he at last succeeded in finding the heart of the Knight of the Swords and, to save his life, destroyed it, thus banishing Arioch to limbo and allowing Arkyn of Law to return to occupy his old castle.

But Corum had earned the bane of the Sword Rulers and by destroying Arioch's heart had set a pattern of destiny for himself. A voice told him: "Neither Law nor Chaos must dominate the destinies of the mortal planes. There must be equilibrium." But it seemed to Corum that there was no equilibrium, that Chaos ruled All. "The Balance sometimes tips," replied the voice. "It must be righted. And that is the power of mortals, to adjust the Balance. You have begun the work already. Now you must continue until it is finished. You may perish before it is complete, but some other will follow you."

Corum shouted: "I do not want this. I cannot bear such a burden."

The voice replied:

"YOU MUST!"

And then Corum returned to find Shool's power gone and Rhalina free.

They returned to the lovely castle on Moidel's Mount, knowing that they were no longer in any sense in control of their own fates...

— *The Book of Corum*

BOOK ONE

IN WHICH PRINCE CORUM MEETS
A POET, HEARS A PORTENT AND
PLANS A JOURNEY

WHAT THE SEA GOD DISCARDED

Now the skies of summer were pale blue over the deeper blue of the sea; over the golden green of the mainland forest; over the grassy rocks of Moidel's Mount and the white stones of the castle raised on its peak. And the last of the Vadhagh race, Prince Corum in the Scarlet Robe, was deep in love with the Mabden woman, Margravine Rhalina of Allomglyl.

Corum Jhaelen Irsei, whose right eye was covered by a patch encrusted with dark jewels so that it resembled the orb of an insect, whose left eye (the natural one) was large and almond-shaped with a yellow centre and purple surround, was unmistakeably Vadhagh. His skull was narrow and long and tapering at the chin and his ears were tapered, too. They had no lobes and were flat against the skull. The hair was fair and finer than the finest Mabden maiden's, his mouth was wide, full-lipped, and his skin was rose-pink and flecked with gold. He would have been handsome save for the baroque blemish that was now his right eye and for the somewhat grim twist to his lips. Then, too, there was the alien hand which strayed often to his sword hilt, visible when he pushed back his scarlet robe.

This left hand bore six fingers on it and seemed encased in a jeweled gauntlet (not so—the 'jewels' were the hand's skin). It was a sinister thing and it had crushed the heart of the Knight of the Swords himself—my lord Arioch of Chaos—and allowed Arkyn, Lord of Law, to return.

Corum certainly seemed a being bent on vengeance and he was, indeed, pledged to avenge his murdered family by slaying Earl Glandyth-a-Krae, servant of King Lyr-a-Brode of Kalenwyr, who ruled the south and the east of the continent once ruled by the Vadhagh. And he was also pledged to the cause of Law against the cause of Chaos (whose servants Lyr and his subjects were). This knowledge made him sober and manly, but it also made his soul heavy. He was also unsettled by the thought of the power grafted to his flesh—the power of the Hand and the Eye.

The Margravine Rhalina was womanly and beautiful and her gentle face was framed by thick, black tresses. She had huge dark eyes and red, loving lips. She, too, was nervous of the sorcerous gifts of the dead wizard Shool, but she tried not to brood upon them, just as earlier she had refused to brood upon the loss of her husband, the Margrave, when he had been drowned in a shipwreck while on his way to Lywm-an-Esh, the land he served and which was gradually being covered by the sea.

She found more to laugh at than did Corum and she was his comfort, for once he had been innocent and had laughed a great deal, and he remembered this innocence with longing. But the longing brought other memories—of his family lying dead, mutilated, dishonoured on the sward outside Castle Erorn as it burned and Glandyth brandished his weapons which were clothed in Vadhagh blood. Such violent images were stronger than the images of his earlier, peaceful life. They forever inhabited his skull, sometimes filling it, sometimes lurking in the darker corners and merely threatening to fill it. And when his revenge-lust seemed to wane, they would always bring it back to fullness. Fire, flesh and fear; the barbaric chariots of the Denledhyssi—brass, iron and crude gold. Short, shaggy horses and burly, bearded warriors in borrowed Vadhagh armour—opening their red mouths and bellowing their insensate triumph, while the old stones of Castle Erorn cracked and tumbled in the yelling blaze and Corum discovered what hate and terror were...

Glandyth's brutal features would fill his dreams, dominating even the dead, tortured faces of his parents and his sisters, so that he would often awake in the middle of the night, fierce, tensed and shouting.

Then only Rhalina could calm him, stroking his ruined face and holding his shaking body close to her own.

Yet, during those days of early summer, there were moments of peace and they could ride through the woods of the mainland without fear, now, of the Pony Tribes who had fled at the sight of the ship Shool had sent on the night of their attack—a dead ship from the bottom of the sea, crewed by corpses and commanded by the dead Margrave himself, Rhalina's drowned husband.

The woods were full of sweet life, of little animals and bright flowers and rich scents. And though they never quite succeeded, they offered to heal the scars on Corum's soul; they offered an alternative to conflict and death and sorcerous horror and they showed him that there were things in the universe which were calm and ordered and beautiful and that Law offered more than just a sterile order but sought to establish throughout the Fifteen Planes a harmony in which all things could exist in all their variety. Law offered an environment in which all the mortal virtues could flourish.

Yet while Glandyth and all he represented survived, Corum knew that Law would be under constant threat and that the corrupting monster Fear would destroy all virtue.

As they rode, one pretty day, through the woods, he cast about him with his mismatched eyes and he said to Rhalina, "Glandyth must die!"

And she nodded but did not question why he had made this sudden statement, for she had heard it many times in similar circumstances. She tightened the rein on her chestnut mare and brought the beast to a prancing halt in a glade of lupines and hollyhocks. She dismounted and picked up her long skirts of embroidered samite as she waded gracefully through the knee-high grass. Corum sat on his tawny stallion and watched her, taking pleasure in her pleasure as she had known he would. The glade was warm and shadowy, sheltered by kindly elm and oak and ash in which squirrels and birds had made their nests.

"Oh, Corum, if only we could stay here for ever! We could build a cottage, plant a garden…"

He tried to smile. "But we cannot," he said. "Even this is but a respite. Shool was right. By accepting the logic of conflict I have accepted a particular destiny. Even if I forgot my own vows of vengeance, even if I had not agreed to serve Law against Chaos, Glandyth would still come and seek us out and make us defend this peace. And Glandyth is stronger than these gentle woods, Rhalina. He could destroy them overnight and, I think, would relish so doing if he knew we loved them."

She knelt and smelled the flowers. "Must it always be so? Must hate always breed hate and love be powerless to proliferate?"

"If Lord Arkyn is right, it will not always be so. But those who believe that love should be powerful must be prepared to die to ensure its strength."

She raised her head suddenly and there was alarm in her eyes as they stared into his.

He shrugged. "It is true," he said.

Slowly, she got to her feet and went back to where her horse stood. She put a foot into the stirrup and pulled herself into the side-saddle. He remained in the same position, staring at the flowers and at the grass which was gradually springing back into the places it had occupied before she had walked through it.

"It is true."

He sighed and turned his horse towards the shore.

"We had best return," he murmured, "before the sea covers the causeway."

A little while later they emerged from the forest and trotted their steeds along the shore. Blue sea shifted on the white sand and, still some distance away, they saw the natural causeway leading through the shallows to the mount on which stood Castle Moidel, the farthest and forgotten outpost of the civilization of Lywm-an-Esh. Once the castle had stood among woods on the mainland of Lywm-an-Esh, but the sea now covered that land.

Seabirds called and wheeled in the cloudless sky, sometimes diving to spear a fish with their beaks and return with their catch to their nests amongst the rocks of Moidel's Mount. The hoofs of the horses thumped the sand or splashed through the surf as they neared the causeway which would soon be covered by the tide.

And then Corum's attention was caught by a movement far out to sea. He craned forward as he rode and peered into the distance.

"What is it?" she asked him.

"I am not sure. A big wave, perhaps. But this is not the season of heavy seas." He pointed. "Look."

"There seems to be a mist hanging over the water a mile or two out. It is hard to observe..." She gasped. "It is a wave!"

Now the water near the shore became slightly more agitated as the wave approached.

"It is as if some huge ship were passing by at great speed," Corum said. "It is familiar…"

Then he looked more sharply into the distant haze. "Do you see something—a shadow—the shadow of a man on the mist?"

"Yes, I do see it. It is enormous. Perhaps an illusion—something to do with the light…"

"No," he said. "I have seen that outline before. It is the giant—the great fisherman who was the cause of my shipwreck on the coast of Khoolocrah!"

"The Wading God," she said. "I know of him. He is sometimes also called the Fisher. Legends say that when he is seen it is an ominous portent."

"It was an ominous enough portent for me when I last saw him," Corum said with some humour. Now good-sized waves were rolling up the beach and they backed their horses off. "He comes closer. Yet the mist follows him."

It was true. The mist was moving nearer the shore as the waves grew larger and the gigantic fisherman waded closer. They could see his outline clearly now. His shoulders were bowed as he hauled his great net, walking backwards through the water.

"What is he thought to catch?" whispered Corum. "Whales? Sea monsters?"

"Anything," she replied. "Anything that is upon or under the sea." She shivered.

The causeway was now completely covered by the artificial tide and there was no point in going forward. They were forced further back towards the trees as the sea rolled in in massive breakers, crashing upon the sand and the shingle.

A little of the mist seemed to touch them and it became cold, though the sun was still bright. Corum drew his cloak about him. There came the steady sound of the giant's strides as he waded on. Somehow he seemed a doomed figure to Corum—a creature destined to drag his nets for ever through the oceans of the world, never finding the thing he sought.

"They say he fishes for his soul," murmured Rhalina. "For his soul."

Now the silhouette straightened its back and hauled in its net. Many creatures struggled there—some of them unrecognizable. The Wading God inspected his catch carefully and then shook out the net, letting the things fall back into the water. He moved on slowly, once again fishing for something it seemed he would never find.

The mist began to leave the shore as the dim outline of the giant moved out to sea again. The waters began to subside until at last they were still and the mist vanished beyond the horizon.

Corum's horse snorted and pawed at the wet sand. The Prince in the Scarlet Robe looked at Rhalina. Her eyes were blank, fixed on the horizon. Her features were rigid.

"The danger is gone," he said, trying to comfort her.

"There was no danger," she said. "It is a warning of danger that the Wading God brings."

"It is only what the legends say."

Her eyes became alive again as she regarded him. "And have we not had cause to believe in legends of late?"

He nodded. "Come, let's get back to the castle before the causeway's flooded a second time."

Their horses were grateful to be moving towards the

sanctuary of Moidel's Castle. The sea was rising swiftly on both sides of the rocky path as they began to cross and the horses broke spontaneously into a gallop.

At last they reached the great gates of the castle and these swung open to admit them. Rhalina's handsome warriors welcomed them back gladly, anxious for their own experiences to be confirmed.

"Did you see the giant, my lady Margravine?" Beldan, her steward, sprang down the steps of the west tower. "I thought it another of Glandyth's allies." The young man's normally cheerful, open face was clouded. "What drove it off?"

"Nothing," she said, dismounting. "It was the Wading God. He was merely going about his business."

Beldan looked relieved. As with all the inhabitants of Castle Moidel, he ever expected a new attack. And he was right in his expectations. Sooner or later Glandyth would march again against the castle, bringing more powerful allies than the superstitious and easily frightened warriors of the Pony Tribes. They had heard that Glandyth, after his failure to take Castle Moidel, had returned in a rage to the Court at Kalenwyr to ask King Lyr-a-Brode for an army. Perhaps next time he came he would also bring ships which could attack from seaward while he attacked from the land. Such an assault would be successful, for Moidel's garrison was small.

The sun was setting as they made for the main hall of the castle to take their evening meal. Corum, Rhalina and Beldan sat together to eat and Corum's mortal hand went often to the wine jug and far less frequently to the food. He was pensive, full of a sense of profound gloom which infected the others so that they did not even attempt to make conversation.

Two hours passed in this way and still Corum swallowed wine. And then Beldan raised his head, listening. Rhalina, too, heard the sound and frowned. Only Corum appeared not to hear it.

It was a rapping noise—an insistent noise. Then there were voices and the rapping stopped for a moment. When the voices subsided the rapping began again.

Beldan got up. "I'll investigate…"

Rhalina glanced at Corum. "I'll stay."

Corum's head was lowered as he stared into his cup, sometimes fingering the patch covering his alien eye, sometimes raising the Hand of Kwll and stretching the six fingers, flexing them, inspecting them, puzzling over the implications of his situation.

Rhalina listened. She heard Beldan's voice. Again the rapping died. There was a further exchange. Silence.

Beldan came back into the hall.

"We have a visitor at our gates," he informed her.

"Where is he from?"

"He says he is a traveler who has suffered some hardship and seeks sanctuary."

"A trick?"

"I know not."

Corum looked up. "A stranger?"

"Aye," Beldan said. "Some spy of Glandyth's possibly."

Corum rose unsteadily. "I'll come to the gate."

Rhalina touched his arm. "Are you sure…?"

"Of course." He passed his hand over his face and drew a deep breath. He began to stride from the hall, Rhalina and Beldan following.

He came to the gates and as he did so the knocking started up once more.

"Who are you?" Corum called. "What business have you with the folk of Moidel's Castle?"

"I am Jhary-a-Conel, a traveler. I am here through no

particular wish of my own, but I would be grateful for a meal and somewhere to sleep."

"Are you of Lywm-an-Esh?" Rhalina asked.

"I am of everywhere and nowhere. I am all men and no man. But one thing I am not—and that is your enemy. I am wet and I am shivering with cold."

"How came you to Moidel when the causeway is covered?" Beldan asked. He turned to Corum. "I have already asked him this once. He did not answer me."

The unseen stranger mumbled something in reply.

"What was that?" Corum said.

"Damn you! It's not a thing a man likes to admit. I was part of a catch of fish! I was brought here in a net and I was dumped offshore and I swam to this damned castle and I climbed your damned rocks and I knocked on your damned door and now I stand making conversation with damned fools. Have you no charity at Moidel?"

The three of them were astonished then—and they were convinced that the stranger was not in league with Glandyth.

Rhalina signed to the warriors to open the great gates. They creaked back a fraction and a slim, bedraggled fellow entered. He was dressed in unfamiliar garb and had a sack over his back, a hat on his head whose wide brim was weighed down by water and hung about his face. His long hair was as wet as the rest of him. He was relatively young, relatively good-looking and, in spite of his sodden appearance, there was just a trace of amused disdain in his intelligent eyes. He bowed to Rhalina.

"Jhary-a-Conel at your service, ma'am."

"How came you to keep your hat while swimming so far through the sea?" Beldan asked. "And your sack, for that matter?"

Jhary-a-Conel acknowledged the question with a wink. "I

never lose my hat and I rarely lose my sack. A traveler of my sort learns to hold on to his few possessions—no matter what circumstances he finds himself in."

"You are just that?" Corum asked. "A traveler?"

Jhary-a-Conel showed some impatience. "Your hospitality reminds me somewhat of that I experienced some time since at a place called Kalenwyr…"

"You have come from Kalenwyr?"

"I have been *to* Kalenwyr. But I see I cannot shame you, even by that comparison…"

"I am sorry," said Rhalina. "Come. There is food already on the table. I'll have servants bring you a change of clothing and towels and so forth."

They returned to the main hall. Jhary-a-Conel looked about him. "Comfortable," he said.

They sat in their chairs and watched him as he casually stripped off his wet clothes and stood at last naked before them. He scratched his nose. A servant brought him towels and he began busily to dry himself. But the new clothes he refused. Instead he wrapped himself in another towel and seated himself at the table, helping himself to food and wine. "I'll take my own clothes when they're dry," he informed the servants. "I have a stupid habit concerning clothes not of my particular choosing. Take care when you dry the hat. The brim must be tilted just so."

These instructions done, he turned to Corum with a bright smile. "And what name is it in this particular time and place, my friend?"

Corum frowned. "I fail to understand you."

"Your name is all I asked. Yours changes as does mine. The difference is sometimes that you do not know that and I do—or vice versa. And sometimes we are the same creature—or, at least, aspects of the same creature."

Corum shook his head. The man sounded mad.

"For instance," continued Jhary as he ate heartily through a piled plate of seafood, "I have been called Timeras and Shalenak. Sometimes I am the hero, but more often than not I am the companion to a hero."

"Your words make little sense, sir," Rhalina said gently. "I do not think Prince Corum understands them. Neither do we."

Jhary grinned. "Ah, then this is one of those times when the hero is aware of only one existence. For the best, I suppose, for it is often unpleasant to remember too many incarnations—particularly when they coexist. I recognize Prince Corum for an old friend, but he does not recognize me. It matters not." He finished his food, readjusted the towel about his waist and leaned back.

"So you'd offer us a riddle and then will not give us the answer," Beldan said.

"I will explain," Jhary told him, "for I do not deliberately jest with you. I am a traveler of an unusual kind. It seems to be my destiny to move through all times and all planes. I do not remember being born and I do not expect to die—in the accepted sense. I am sometimes called Timeras and, if I am 'of' anywhere, then I suppose I am of Tanelorn."

"But Tanelorn is a myth," said Beldan.

"All places are a myth somewhere else—but Tanelorn is more constant than most. She can be found, if sought, from anywhere in the multiverse."

"Have you no profession?" Corum asked him.

"Well, I have made some poetry and plays in my time, but my main profession could be that I am a friend of heroes. I have travelled—under several names, of course, and in several guises—with Rackhir the Red Archer to Xerlerenes where the ships of the Boatmen sail the skies as your ships sail the sea—with Elric of Melniboné to the Court of the Dead God—with Asquiol of Pompeii into the deeper reaches of the multiverse where space is measured not in terms of miles but in terms of galaxies—with Hawkmoon of Köln to Londra where the folk wear jeweled masks fashioned into the faces of beasts. I have seen the future and the past. I have seen a variety of planetary systems and I have learned that time does not exist and that space is an illusion."

"And the gods?" Corum asked him eagerly.

"I think we create them, but I am not sure. Where primitives invent crude gods to explain the thunder, more sophisticated peoples create more elaborate gods to explain the abstractions which puzzle them. It has often been noted that gods could not exist without mortals and mortals could not exist without gods."

"Yet gods, it appears," said Corum, "can affect our destinies."

"And we can affect theirs, can we not?"

Beldan murmured to Corum, "Your own experiences are proof of that, Prince Corum."

"So you can wander at will amongst the Fifteen Planes," Corum said softly. "As some Vadhagh once could."

Jhary smiled. "I can wander nowhere 'at will'—or to very few places. I can sometimes return to Tanelorn, if I wish, but normally I am hurled from one existence to another without, apparently, rhyme or reason. I usually find that I am made to fulfill my rôle wherever I land up—which is to be a companion to champions, the friend of heroes. That is why I recognized you at once for what you are—the Champion Eternal. I have known him in many forms, but he has not always known me. Perhaps, in my own periods of amnesia, I have not always known him."

"And are you never a hero yourself?"

"I have been heroic, I suppose, as some would see it. Perhaps I have even been a hero of sorts. And, there again, it is sometimes my fate to be one aspect of a particular hero—a part of another man or group of other men who together make up a single great hero. The stuff of our identities is blown by a variety of winds—all of them whimsical—about the multiverse. There is even a theory I have heard that all mortals are aspects of one single cosmic identity and some believe that even the gods are part of that identity, that all the planes of existence, all the ages which come and go, all the manifestations of space which emerge and vanish, are merely ideas in this cosmic mind, different fragments of its personality. Such speculation leads us nowhere and everywhere, but it makes no difference to our understanding of our immediate problems."

"I'd agree with that," Corum told him feelingly. "And now, will you explain in more detail how you came to Moidel?"

"I will explain what I can, friend Corum. It happened that I found myself at a grim place called Kalenwyr. How I came there I do not quite remember, but then I am used to that. This Kalenwyr—all granite and gloom—was not to my taste. I was there but a few hours before I came under suspicion of the inhabitants and, by means of a certain amount of climbing about on roofs, the theft of a chariot, the purloining of a boat on a nearby river, escaped them and reached the sea. Feeling it unsafe to land, I sailed along the coast. A mist closed in, the sea acted as if a storm had blown up and suddenly my boat and myself were caught up with a motley mixture of fish, snapping monsters, men and creatures I would be hard put to describe. I managed to cling to the strands of the gigantic net which had trapped me and the rest as we were dragged along at great speed. How I found breath sometimes I do not remember. Then, at last, the net was upended and we were all released. My companions went their different ways and I was left alone in the water. I saw this island and your castle and I found a piece of driftwood which aided me to swim here…"

"Kalenwyr!" Beldan said. "In Kalenwyr did you hear of a man called Glandyth-a-Krae?"

Jhary frowned. "An Earl Glandyth was mentioned in a tavern, I think—with some admiration. A mighty warrior, I gathered. The whole city seemed preparing for war, but I did not understand the issues or what they considered their enemies. I think they spoke of the land of Lywm-an-Esh with a certain amount of loathing. And they were expecting allies from across the sea."

"Allies? From the Nhadragh Isles, perhaps?" Corum asked him.

"No. I think they spoke of Bro-an-Mabden."

"The continent in the west!" Rhalina gasped. "I did not know many Mabden still inhabited it. But what moves them to plan war against Lywm-an-Esh?"

"Perhaps the same spirit which led them to destroy my race," Corum suggested. "Envy—and a hatred of peace. Your people, you told me, adopted many Vadhagh customs. That would be enough to win them the enmity of Glandyth and his kind."

"It is true," Rhalina said. "Then this means that we are not the only ones who are in danger. Lywm-an-Esh has not fought a war for a hundred years or more. She will be unprepared for this invasion."

A servant brought in Jhary's clothes. They were clean and dry. Jhary thanked him and began to don them, as unselfconsciously as he had taken them off. His shirt was of bright blue silk, his flared pantaloons were as bright a scarlet as Corum's robe. He tied a big yellow sash about his waist and over this buckled a sword belt from which hung a scabbarded sabre and a long poignard. He pulled on soft boots which reached the knee and tied a scarf about his throat. His dark blue cloak he placed on the bench beside him, together with his hat (which he carefully creased to suit his taste) and his bundle. He seemed satisfied. "You had best tell me all you think I need to know," he suggested. "Then I may be able to help you. I have gathered a great deal of information in my travels—most of it useless…"

Corum told him of the Sword Rulers and the Fifteen Planes, of the struggle between Law and Chaos and the attempts to bring equilibrium to the Cosmic Balance. Jhary-a-Conel listened to all of this and seemed familiar with many of the things of which Corum spoke.

When Corum had finished, Jhary said, "It is plain that attempts to contact Lord Arkyn for help would, at this moment, be unsuccessful. Arioch's logic still prevails on these five planes and must be completely demolished before Arkyn and Law can know real power. It is ever the lot of mortals to symbolize these struggles between the gods and doubtless this war which seems likely between King Lyr-a-Brode and Lywm-an-Esh will mirror the war between Law and Chaos on other planes. If those who serve Chaos win—if King Lyr-a-Brode's army wins, in fact—then Lord Arkyn may yet again lose his power and Chaos will triumph. Arioch is not the most powerful of the Sword Rulers—Xiombarg has greater power on the planes she rules and Mabelode has even more power than Xiombarg. I would say that you have hardly experienced the real manifestations of Chaos's rule here."

"You do not comfort me," said Corum.

"It is perhaps better, however, to understand these things," Rhalina said.

"Can the other Sword Rulers send aid to King Lyr?" Corum asked.

"Not directly. But there are ways of manipulating these

things through messengers and agents. Would you know more of Lyr's plans?"

"Of course," Corum told him. "But that is impossible."

Jhary smiled. "I think you will discover that it is useful to have a companion to champions as experienced as myself in your employ." And he stopped and reached into his bag.

He brought something out of the sack which, to their astonishment, was alive. It seemed unruffled by the fact that it had spent a day at least inside the sack. It opened its large, calm eyes and it purred.

It was a cat. Or, at least, it was a kind of cat, for this cat had resting on its back a pair of beautiful black wings tipped with white. Its other markings were black and white, like those of an ordinary cat, with white paws and a white muzzle and a white front. It seemed friendly and self-possessed. Jhary offered it food from the table and the cat ruffled its wings and began to eat hungrily.

Rhalina sent a servant for milk and when the little animal had finished drinking it sat beside Jhary on the bench and began to clean itself, first its face, paws and body and then its wings.

"I have never seen such an animal!" Beldan muttered.

"And I have never seen another like it in all my travels," Jhary agreed. "It is a friendly creature and has often aided me. Sometimes our ways part and I do not see it for an age or two, but we are often together and he always remembers me. I call him Whiskers. Not an original name, I fear, but he seems to like it well enough. I think he will help us now."

"How can he help us?" Corum stared at the winged cat.

"Why, my friends, he can fly to Lyr's Court and witness what takes place there. Then he can return with his news to us!"

"He can speak?"

"Only to me—and even that is not speaking as such. Would you have me send him there?"

Corum was completely taken aback. He was forced to smile. "Why not?"

"Then Whiskers and I will go up to your battlements, with your permission, and I will instruct him what to do."

In silence the three watched Jhary adjust his hat on his head, pick up his cat, bow to them and mount the stairs that would take him to the battlements.

"I feel as if I dream," said Beldan when Jhary had disappeared.

"You do," said Corum. "A fresh dream is just beginning. Let us hope we survive it…"

THE GATHERING AT KALENWYR

THE LITTLE WINGED cat flew swiftly eastward through the night and came at last to gloomy Kalenwyr.

The smoke of a thousand guttering brands rose up from Kalenwyr and seemed to smear out the light of the moon. Square blocks of dark granite made up the houses and the castles and nowhere was there a curve or a soft line. Dominating the rest of the city was the brooding pile of King Lyr-a-Brode and around its black battlements flickered oddly coloured lights and there was a rumbling like thunder, though no clouds filled the night sky.

Towards this pile now flew the little cat, alighting on a tower of harsh angles and folding its wings. It turned its large, green eyes this way and that, as if deciding which way it would enter the castle.

The cat's fur prickled, the long whiskers for which it had been named twitched, the tail went stiff. The cat had become aware not only of sorcery and the presence of supernatural creatures in the castle, but of a particular creature which it hated more than all the rest. Its progress down the side of the tower became even more cautious. It reached a slotted window and squeezed in. It was in a darkened, circular room. An open door revealed steps winding down the inside of the tower. Tensely the cat made its way down the steps. There were plenty of shadows in which to hide, for Castle Kalenwyr was a shadowy place.

At last the cat saw brandlight burning ahead and it paused, looking warily around the door frame. The brands illuminated a long, narrow passage and at the end of the passage were the sounds of many voices, the clatter of arms and of wine-cups. The cat spread its wings and flew into the shadows of the roof, finding a long, blackened beam down which it could walk. The beam passed through the wall with a little room to spare and the cat squeezed through to find itself looking down at a huge gathering of Mabden. It walked further along the beam and then settled itself to watch the proceedings.

In the centre of Castle Kalenwyr's Great Hall was a dais carved from a single block of unpolished obsidian and upon this dais was a throne of granite studded with quartz. Some attempt had been made to carve gargoyles upon the stone, but the workmanship was crude and unfinished. Nonetheless, the half-shapes carved there were more sinister than if they had been fully realized.

Seated upon this throne were three people. On each asymmetrical arm sat a naked girl, with flesh tattooed in obscene designs. Each girl held a jug with which she replenished the wine-cup of the man who sat on the throne itself. This man was big—more than seven feet tall—and a crown of pale iron was upon his matted hair. The hair was long, with short plaits clustered over the forehead. It had been yellow but was now streaked with white and it seemed that some attempt had been made to dye these streaks back to their original colour. The beard, too, was yellow and flecked with areas of stained grey. The face was haggard, covered in broken veins, and from the deep eye-sockets peered eyes that were bloodshot, faded blue, full of hatred, cunning and suspicion. Robes clothed the body from neck to foot. These were plainly of Vadhagh origin—brocades and samite now covered in the marks of food and wine. Over them was thrown a dirty coat of tawny wolfskin—just as plainly made by the Mabden of the east, whom the man ruled. The hands were encrusted with stolen rings torn from the fingers of slain Vadhagh and Nhadragh. One of the hands rested upon the pommel of a great, battered iron sword. The other clutched a bronze, diamond-studded goblet from which slopped thick wine. Surrounding the dais, their backs to their master, was a guard of warriors each as tall or taller than the man on the throne. They stood rigidly shoulder to shoulder, swords drawn and placed across the rims of their great oval shields of leather and iron sheathed in brass. Their brass helms covered most of their faces and from the sides escaped the hair of their heads and beards. Their eyes seemed to contain a perpetual and controlled fury and they looked steadily into the middle distance. This was the Asper Guard—the Grim Guard which was unthinkingly loyal to the man who sat upon the throne.

King Lyr-a-Brode turned his massive head and surveyed his Court.

Warriors filled it.

The only women were the tattooed, naked wenches who served the wine. Their hair was dirty, their bodies bruised and they moved like dead things with their heavy wine jugs balanced on their hips, squeezing themselves in and out of the ranks of the big, brutal Mabden men in their barbaric war-gear, with their braided hair and beards.

These men stank of sweat and of the blood they had spilled. Their leather clothes creaked as they raised wine-cups to their hard mouths, their harness rattled.

A feast had recently taken place here, but now the tables and the benches had been cleared away and, save for the few who had collapsed and been dragged into corners, all the warriors were standing, watching their king and waiting for him to speak.

The light from iron braziers suspended from the roof beams flung their huge shadows on the dark stone and made their eyes shine red like the eyes of beasts.

Each warrior in the hall was a commander of other warriors. Here were earls and dukes and counts and captains who had ridden from all parts of Lyr's kingdom to attend this gathering. And some, dressed a little differently from the others, favouring fur to the stolen Vadhagh and Nhadragh samite, had come from across the sea as emissaries from Bro-an-Mabden, the rocky land of the north-west from which the whole Mabden race had originated long ago.

Now King Lyr-a-Brode placed his hands on the arms of his throne and levered himself slowly to his feet. Instantly five hundred arms raised goblets in a toast.

"LYR OF THE LAND!"

Automatically he returned the toast, mumbling, "And the Land is Lyr..." He looked around him, almost disbelievingly, staring for a long second at one of the girls as if he recognized her for something other than she was. He frowned.

A burly noble with grey, unhealthy eyes, a red, shiny face, his thick black hair and beard curled and braided, a cruel mouth which was partly closed over yellow fangs, stepped from the throng and positioned himself just the other side of the Grim Guard. This noble wore a tall, winged helmet of iron, brass and gold, a huge bearskin cloak on his shoulders. There was a sense of authority about him and, in many ways, he had more presence than did the tall king who looked down on him.

The king's lips moved. "Earl Glandyth-a-Krae?"

"My liege, I hight Glandyth, Earl over the estates of Krae," the man assured him formally. "Captain of the Denledhyssi who have scoured your land free of the Vadhagh vermin and all who allied themselves with them, who helped conquer the Nhadragh Isles. And I am a Brother of the Dog, a Son of the Horned Bear, a servant of the Lords of Chaos!"

King Lyr nodded. "I know thee, Glandyth. A loyal sword."

Glandyth bowed.

There was a pause.

Then, "Speak," said the king.

"There is one of the Shefanhow creatures who escapes your justice, my king. Just one Vadhagh who still lives." Glandyth tugged the thong of his jerkin which showed over the top of his breastplate. He reached inside and brought out two things which hung by a string around his neck. One of the things was a withered, mummified hand. The other was a small leather pouch. He displayed them. "This is the hand I cut from the Vadhagh and here, in this sack, is his eye. He took refuge in the castle which lies at the far western shore of your land—the castle called Moidel. A Mabden woman possessed that castle—she is the Margravine Rhalina-a-Allomglyl and she serves that land of traitors, Lywm-an-Esh—that land which you now plan to crush because it refuses to support our cause."

"All this you have told me," King Lyr replied. "And you have told me of the monstrous sorcery used to thwart your attack upon that castle. Speak on."

"I would march again to Castle Moidel, for I have learned that the Shefanhow Corum and the traitress Rhalina have returned there, thinking themselves safe from your justice."

"All our armies go westward," Lyr told him. "All our strength is aimed at the destruction of Lywm-an-Esh. Castle Moidel will fall in our passing."

"The boon I beg is that I be the instrument of that fall, my liege."

"You are one of our greatest captains, Earl Glandyth, we would use you and your Denledhyssi in a main engagement."

"While Corum lives, commanding sorcery, our cause is much threatened. I speak truly, great king. He is a powerful enemy— perhaps more powerful than the whole land of Lywm-an-Esh. It will take much to destroy him."

"One maimed Shefanhow? How is this so?"

"He has made an alliance with Law. I have proof. One of my Nhadragh lackeys has used its second sight and seen clear."

"Where is the Nhadragh?"

"He is without, my liege. I would not bring the vile creature into your hall without your permission."

"Bring him now."

All the bearded warriors stared towards the door with a mixture of disgust and curiosity. Only the Grim Guard did not turn its gaze. King Lyr reseated himself on his throne and gestured with his cup for more wine.

The doors were opened and a dim shape was revealed. Though it had the outline of a man it was not a man. The ranks broke as it began to shuffle forward.

It had dark, flat features and the hair of its head grew down its forehead to meet at a peak just below the eyebrows. It was dressed in a jacket and breeks of sealskin. Its stance was servile, nervous and it bowed frequently as it moved towards the waiting Glandyth.

King Lyr-a-Brode's lips curled in nausea. He gestured at Glandyth. "Make this thing speak and then make it leave."

Glandyth reached out and seized the Nhadragh by his coarse hair. "Now, filth, tell my king what you saw with your degenerate senses!"

The Nhadragh opened its mouth and stuttered.

"Speak! Quickly!"

"I—I saw into other planes than this…"

"You saw into Yffarn—into hell?" King Lyr murmured in horror.

"Into other planes…" The Nhadragh looked shiftily about him and agreed hastily. "Aye, then—into Yffarn. I saw a creature there which I cannot describe, but I spoke with it for a brief time. It— told me that Lord Arioch of Chaos…"

"He means the Sword Ruler," Glandyth explained. "He means Arag the Great Old God."

"It told me that Arioch—Arag—had been slain by Corum Jhaelen Irsei of the Vadhagh and that Lord Arkyn of Law now ruled these five planes again…" The Nhadragh's voice trailed off.

"Tell my king the rest," Glandyth said fiercely, tugging again on the wretch's hair. "Tell him what you learned relating to us Mabden!"

"I was told that now Lord Arkyn has returned he will attempt to regain all the power he once had over the world. But he needs mortals as his agents and of these agents Corum is the most important—but it is certain that most of the folk of Lywm-an-Esh will serve Arkyn, too, for they learned the ways of the—the Shefanhow—long since…"

"So all our suspicions were correct," King Lyr said in quiet triumph. "We do well to ready for war against Lywm-an-Esh. We fight against that soft degeneration misnamed as Law!"

"And you would agree that it is my duty to destroy this Corum?" Glandyth asked.

The king frowned. Then he raised his head and looked directly at Glandyth. "Aye." He waved his hand. "Now take that stinking Shefanhow from this hall. It is time to summon the Dog and the Bear!"

High on the central roof beam the little cat felt its fur stiffen. It was inclined to leave the hall there and then, but made itself stay. It was loyal to its master and Jhary-a-Conel had told it to witness all that passed during Lyr's gathering.

Now the warriors had packed themselves around the walls. The women had been dismissed. Lyr himself left his throne and the whole centre of the hall was now barren of men.

A silence fell.

Lyr clapped his hands from where he stood, still surrounded by his Grim Guard.

The doors of the hall opened and prisoners were brought in. There were young children and women and some men of the peasant class. All were comely and all were terrified. They were wheeled into the hall in a great wicker cage and some of the children were wailing. The imprisoned adults made no attempt to comfort the children any longer, but clutched at the wicker bars and stared hopelessly out into the hall.

"Aha!" King Lyr cried. "Here is the food of the Dog and the Bear. Tender food! Tasty food!" He relished their misery. He stepped forward and the Grim Guard stepped forward too. He licked his lips as he inspected the prisoners. "Let the food be cooked," he commanded, "so that the smell will reach into Yffarn and whet the appetites of the gods and draw them to us."

One of the women began to scream and some of them fainted. Two of the young men bowed their heads and wept and the children looked out of their cage uncomprehendingly, merely frightened by the fact of their imprisonment, not of the fate which was to come.

Ropes were passed through loops at the top of the cage and men hauled on the ropes so that the entire contraption was raised towards the roof beams.

The little cat shifted its position, but continued to observe.

A huge brazier was wheeled in next and placed directly below the cage. The cage rocked and swayed as the prisoners struggled. The eyes of the watching warriors glowed in anticipation. The brazier was full of white-hot coals and now servants came with jars of oil and flung it upon the coals so that flames suddenly roared high into the air and licked around the wicker cage. A horrid ululation came from the cage then—a dreadful, incoherent noise which filled the hall.

And King Lyr-a-Brode began to laugh.

Glandyth-a-Krae began to laugh.

The earls and the counts and the dukes and the captains of his Court all began to laugh.

And soon the screams subsided and were replaced by the crackling of the fire, the smell of roasting human flesh.

Then the laughter died and silence came again to the hall as the warriors waited tensely to see what would happen next.

Somewhere beyond the walls of Castle Kalenwyr—somewhere out beyond the town—beyond the darkness of the night—there came a howling.

The little cat drew itself further back along the beam, close to the opening which led into the passage beyond the hall.

The howling grew louder and the flames of the great brazier seemed to be chilled by it and went out.

Now there was pitch darkness in the hall.

The howling echoed everywhere, rising and falling, sometimes seeming to die and then rising to an even louder pitch.

And then it was joined by a peculiar roaring sound.

These were the sounds of the Dog and the Bear—the dark and dreadful gods of the Mabden.

The hall shuddered. A peculiar light began to manifest itself over the vacant throne.

And then, wreathed in radiance of unpleasant and unnameable colours, a being stood on the granite dais and it turned its muzzle this way and that, sniffing for the feast. It was huge and it stank and it stood upon its hind legs like a parody of those who, quaking, observed it.

The Dog sniffed again. Noises came from its throat. It shook its hairy head.

Still from somewhere came the other sound—the sound of grunting and roaring. This now grew louder and louder and, hearing it, the Dog cocked its head on one side and paused in its sniffing.

A dark blue light appeared on the dais on the opposite side of the throne. It took a form and the Bear stood there—a great, black bear with long, black horns curling from its head. It opened its snout and grimaced, displaying its pointed fangs. It reached out towards the charred wicker cage and it ripped it down from where it hung.

The Dog and the Bear fell upon the contents of the cage, stuffing the roasted human flesh into their mouths, growling and snuffling and choking, crunching the bones with the bloody juices running down their snouts.

And then they were finished and they lounged on the dais and glared around them at the silent, fearful mortals.

Primitive gods for a primitive people.

For the first time King Lyr-a-Brode left his circle of guards and walked towards the throne. He lowered himself to his knees and raised his arms in supplication to the Dog and the Bear.

"Great lords, hear us!" he moaned. "We have learned that Lord Arag has been slain by our enemy the Shefanhow who is in league with our enemies of Lywm-an-Esh, the Sinking Land. Our cause is threatened and thus is your own rule in danger. Will you aid us, lords?"

The Dog growled. The Bear snuffled.

"Will you aid us, lords?"

The Dog cast its fierce eyes about the hall and it seemed that the same feral glint was in every other eye there. It was pleased. It spoke.

"We know of the danger. It is greater than you think." The voice was clipped, harsh and it did not come easily to the canine throat. "You will have to marshal your strength quickly and march swiftly upon our enemies if those we serve are to retain their power and make you, in turn, stronger."

"Our captains are already gathered, my lord the Dog, and their armies come to join them at Kalenwyr."

"That is good. Then we shall send you the aid we can send."
The Dog turned its huge head and regarded its brother the Bear.

The Bear's voice was high-pitched but easier to understand.

"Our enemies will also seek aid, but they will have greater difficulty in finding it, for Arkyn of Law is still weak. Arioch—whom you call Arag—must be brought back to his rightful place to rule these planes again. But if he is to do this a new heart must be found for him and a new fleshly form. There is only one heart and one form which will serve—the heart and form of his banisher, Corum in the Scarlet Robe. Complicated sorcery will be required to prepare Corum once he is captured—but captured he must be."

"Not slain?"

It was Glandyth's disappointed tones.

"Why spare him?" said the Bear.

And even Glandyth shuddered.

"We leave now," said the Dog. "Our aid will arrive soon. It will be led by one who is a messenger to the Great Gods themselves—to the Sword Ruler of the next plane, Queen Xiombarg. He will tell you more than can we."

And then the Dog and the Bear were gone and the stink of the cooked human flesh hung in the black hall and King Lyr's quaking voice called through the darkness. "Bring brands! Bring brands!"

The doors were opened and a dim, reddish light fell down the middle of the hall. It showed the dais, the throne, the torn wicker cage, the extinguished brazier, and the kneeling, shuddering king.

Lyr-a-Brode's eyes rolled as he was helped to his feet by two of his Grim Guards. He did not seem to relish the responsibility which his gods had implied was his. He looked almost pleadingly at Glandyth.

And Glandyth was grinning and Glandyth was panting like a dog about to feast on fresh-caught prey.

The little cat crept down the beam, along the passage, up the stairs to the tower. And it went away on weary wings, back to Castle Moidel.

3

LYWM-AN-ESH

I T WAS A still, warm afternoon in high summer and a few wisps of white cloud lay close to the horizon. Bright, gentle blossoms stretched across the sward for as far as the eye could see, growing right down to where the yellow sand divided the land from the flat, calm ocean. All the flowers were wild, but their profusion and variety gave the impression that they had once been planted as part of a vast garden which had been left untended for many years.

Just recently a small, trim schooner had beached on the sand and out of it had emerged a bright company, leading horses down makeshift gangplanks. Silks and steel flashed in the sunlight as the whole complement abandoned the craft, mounted its steeds and began to move inland.

The four leading riders reached the sward and their horses moved knee-deep through wild tulips as soft and richly coloured as velvet. The riders took deep breaths of the marvelously scented air.

All save one of the riders were armoured. One, tall and strange-featured, wore a jeweled patch over his right eye and a six-fingered jeweled gauntlet upon his left hand. He had a high, conical helm, apparently of silver, with an aventail of tiny silver links suspended from staples round the lower edge of the helm. His byrnie was also of silver, although its second layer was of brass, and his shirt, breeks and boots were of soft brushed leather. He had a long sword at his side, its pommel and guard decorated with delicate silverwork as well as red-and-black onyx. In a saddle sheath was a long-hafted war-axe with decorations matching those on the sword. On his back was a coat of a peculiar texture and of brilliant scarlet and on this were crossed a quiver of arrows and a long bow. This was Prince Corum Jhaelen Irsei in the Scarlet Robe, caparisoned for war.

Next to Prince Corum rode one who also wore mail, though with an elaborate helm fashioned from the shell of the giant murex and with a shield which was also made from shell. A slender sword and a lance were the weapons of this rider and she was the beautiful Margravine Rhalina of Allomglyl, caparisoned for war.

At Rhalina's side rode a handsome young man with a helm and shield that matched hers, a tall lance and a short-hafted war-axe, a sword and a long, broad-bladed baselard. His long cloak was of orange samite and matched the sleek coat of his chestnut mare whose jeweled harness was probably worth more than the rider's own gear. And this was Beldan-an-Allomglyl, caparisoned for war.

The fourth rider wore a broad-brimmed hat which was somewhat fastidiously tilted on his head and which now sported a long plume. His shirt was of bright blue silk and his pantaloons rivaled the scarlet of Corum's cloak, there was a broad yellow sash about his waist with a well-worn leather sword belt supporting a sabre and a poignard. His boots reached to the knee and his long, dark blue cloak was so long that it stretched out to cover the whole of his horse's rump. A small black-and-white cat was perched upon his shoulder, its wings folded. It was purring and seemed to be an animal of singularly pleasant disposition. The rider occasionally reached up to stroke its head and murmur to it. And this was the sometime traveler, sometime poet, sometime companion to champions Jhary-a-Conel and he was not seriously caparisoned for war.

Behind them came Rhalina's men-at-arms and their women. The soldiers wore the uniform of Allomglyl, with helms, shields and breastplates made from the gigantic crustaceans that had once populated the sea.

It was a handsome company and it blended well with the landscape of the Duchy of Bedwilral-nan-Rywm, most easterly county in the land of Lywm-an-Esh.

They had left Castle Moidel behind them after a vain attempt had been made to awaken the huge bats that slept in the caves below the castle ("Chaos creatures," Jhary-a-Conel had murmured, "they'll be hard to press into our service now.") and Lord Arkyn, doubtless concerned with more pressing matters, had failed to answer their call to him. It had become plain that Castle Moidel could no longer be defended, when the winged cat had brought back its news, and they had decided to ride all together to the capital of Lywm-an-Esh which was called Halwyg-nan-Vake and warn the king of the coming of the barbarians from the east and the south.

As he looked around him Corum was impressed by the beauty of the landscape and thought he could understand how such a lovely land had produced in a Mabden race so many characteristics he would normally call Vadhagh.

It was not cowardice which had made them abandon Moidel's Mount but it was caution and the knowledge that Glandyth would waste many days—perhaps weeks—by planning and launching an attack on the castle they no longer occupied.

The main city of the Duchy was called Llarak-an-Fol and it would be a good two days' ride before they reached it. Here they hoped to get fresh horses and some information concerning the present state of the country's defenses. The duke himself lived in Llarak and had known Rhalina as a girl. She was certain he would help them and that he would believe the tale they brought. Halwyg-nan-Vake lay another week's ride, at least, beyond Llarak.

Corum, although he had suggested much of their present plan, could not rid from his head some sense that he was retreating from the object of his hatred and part of him wanted to turn back to Moidel and wait for Glandyth's coming. He fought the impulse but the conflict in him often made him gloomy and a poor companion.

The others were more cheerful, delighting in the fact that they were able to help Lywm-an-Esh prepare for an attack which King Lyr-a-Brode thought would be unexpected. With superior weapons, there was every chance of the invasion being completely thwarted.

Only Jhary-a-Conel sometimes had the task of reminding Rhalina and Beldan of the fact that the Dog and the Bear had promised aid to King Lyr, though none knew what form that aid would take and how powerful it would be.

They camped that night on the Plain of Blossoms and by the next morning had reached rolling downlands. Beyond the downs, sheltered by them, lay Llarak-an-Fol.

Then, in the afternoon, they came to a pleasant village built on both sides of a pretty stream and they saw that the village square was full of people who stood around a water trough upon which was balanced a man in dark robes who addressed them.

They reined in on the slope of the hill and watched from a distance, unable to make anything of the babble they heard.

Jhary-a-Conel frowned. "They seem rather agitated. Do you think we are late with our news?"

Corum fingered his eye-patch and considered the scene. "Doubtless nothing more than some local village affair, Jhary. Let's you and I ride down there and ask them."

Jhary nodded and, after a word with the others, they rode rapidly towards the village.

Now the dark-robed man had seen them and their company and he was pointing and shouting. The villagers were plainly disturbed.

As they entered the village street and drew close to the crowd, the dark-robed man, whose face was full of madness, screamed at them. "Who are you? On which side do you fight? Do you come to destroy us? We have nothing for your army."

"Hardly an army," murmured Jhary. Then more loudly he called, "We mean you no harm, friend. We are passing this way on our journey to Llarak."

"To Llarak. So you are on the duke's side! You will help bring disaster on us all!"

"By what means?" Corum called.

"By leaguing yourselves with the forces of weakness—with the soft, degenerate ones who speak of peace and who will bring terrible war to us."

"You are still not especially specific," Jhary said. "Who are you, sir?"

"I am Verenak and I am a priest of Urleh. Thus I serve this

village and have its well-being at stake—not to say the well-being of our entire nation."

Corum whispered to Jhary: "Urleh is a local godling of these parts—a sort of vassal deity to Arioch. I should have thought that his power would have disappeared when Arioch was banished."

"Perhaps that is why this Verenak is so upset," suggested Jhary with a wink.

"Perhaps."

Verenak was now peering closely at Corum. "You are not human!"

"I am mortal," Corum told him equably, "but I am not of the Mabden race, it is true."

"You are Vadhagh!"

"That I am. The last."

Verenak put a trembling hand to his face. He turned again to the villagers. "Drive these two out from here lest the Lords of Chaos take their vengeance upon us! Chaos will soon come and you must be loyal to Urleh if you would survive!"

"Urleh no longer exists," said Corum. "He is banished from our planes with his master Arioch."

"It is a lie!" screamed Verenak. "Urleh lives!"

"It is not likely," Jhary told him.

Corum spoke to the villagers. "Lord Arkyn of Law rules the Five Planes now. He will bring peace to you and a greater security than you have ever previously known."

"Nonsense!" Verenak shouted. "Arkyn was defeated by Arioch ages since."

"And now Arioch is defeated," Corum said. "We must defend this new peace we are offered. Chaos in all its power brings destruction and terror. Your land is threatened by invaders of your own race who serve Chaos and plan to slay you all!"

"I say that you lie—you seek to turn us against the Great Lord

Arioch and the Lord Urleh. We are loyal to Chaos!"

The villagers did not seem to be as certain of that statement as Verenak.

"Then you will bring only disaster to yourselves," Corum insisted. "I know that Arioch is banished—I am the one who sent him into limbo. I destroyed his heart."

"Blasphemy!" shrieked Verenak. "Begone from here. I will not let you corrupt these innocent souls."

The villagers glanced suspiciously at Corum and then bestowed the same suspicious looks upon Verenak. One of them stepped forward. "We have no particular interest in either Law or Chaos," he said. "We wish only to live our lives as we have always lived them. Until recently, Verenak, you did not interfere with us, save to offer us a little magical advice from time to time and receive payment in return. Now you speak of great causes and of struggles and terror. You say that we must arm ourselves and march against our liege the duke. Now this stranger, this Vadhagh, says we must ally ourselves with Law—also to save ourselves. And yet there is no threat that we can see. There have been no portents, Verenak..."

Verenak raged. "There have been signs. They have come to me in dreams. We must become warriors on the side of Chaos, attack Llarak, show that we are loyal to Urleh!"

Corum shrugged. "You must not side with Chaos," he said. "If you would side with no-one, then Chaos will devour you, however. You call our little band an army—and that means you have no conception of what an army can be. Unless we prepare against your enemies your flowery hills will one day be black with riders who will trample you as easily as they trample the blossoms. I have suffered at their hands and I know that they torture and they rape before slaying. Nothing will be left of your village unless you come with us to Llarak and learn how to defend your lovely land."

"How came this dispute to begin?" Jhary asked, taking a different tack. "Why are you trying to arouse these people against the duke, Sir Verenak?"

Verenak glowered. "Because the duke has gone mad. Not a month since he banished all the priests of Urleh from his city but allowed the priests of that milk-and-water godling Ilah to remain. Thus he put himself upon the side of Law and ceased to tolerate the adherents of Chaos. He will therefore bring Urleh's vengeance—aye, even Arioch's vengeance—upon himself. And that is why I seek to warn these poor, simple people and get them to take action."

"The people seem considerably more intelligent than you, my friend," laughed Jhary.

Verenak raised his arms to the skies. "Oh, Urleh, destroy this grinning fool!"

He lost his footing on the water trough's sides. His arms began to wave. He fell backwards into the water. The villagers laughed. The one who had spoken came up to Corum. "Worry not, my friend— we'll do no marching here. We've our crops to harvest, for one thing."

"You'll harvest no crops if the Mabden of the east come this way," Corum warned him. "But I'll debate no longer with you save to warn you that we Vadhagh could not believe in the bloodlust of those Mabden and we ignored the warnings. That is why I saw my father and my mother and my sisters all slain. That is why I am the last of my race."

The man drew his hand over his brow and scratched his head. "I will think on what you have said, friend Vadhagh."

"And what of him?" Corum pointed at Verenak who was hauling himself from the trough.

"He'll bother us no more. He has many villages to visit with his gloomy news. I doubt if many will even take the trouble to listen to him as we have done."

Corum nodded. "Very well, but please remember that these minor disputes, these little arguments, these apparently meaningless decisions like that of the duke in banishing the priests of Urleh, they are all indications that a greater struggle is to come between Law and Chaos. Verenak senses it just as much as does the duke. Verenak seeks to gather strength for Chaos while the duke puts himself in the Camp of Law. Neither knows that a threat is coming, but both have sensed something. And I bring news to Lywm-an-Esh that a struggle is about to begin. Take heed of that warning, my friend. Think of what I have said, no matter how you choose to act upon it..."

The villager sucked at a tooth. "I will think on it," he agreed at last.

The rest of the villagers were going about their business. Verenak was making for his tethered horse, casting many a glowering glance back at Corum.

"Would you and your company take the hospitality of our village?" the man asked Corum.

Corum shook his head. "I thank you, but what I have seen and heard here confirms that we must make speed to Llarak-an-Fol and release our news. Farewell!"

"Farewell, friend." The villager still looked thoughtful.

As they rode back up the hill Jhary was laughing. "As good a comic scene as any I've written for the stage in my time," he said.

"Yet it has tragedy beneath it," Corum told him.

"As does all good comedy."

* * *

And now the company galloped where before it had trotted, riding across the Duchy of Bedwilral-nan-Rywm as if the warriors of Lyr-a-Brode were already pursuing them.

And there was tension in the air. In every village they passed through there were apparently meaningless disputes between neighbours as one side supported Urleh and the other Ilah, but both refused to listen to what Corum told them—that the instruments of Chaos would soon be upon their land and they would cease to exist unless they prepared to resist King Lyr and his armies.

And when they came at last to Llarak-an-Fol, they found that there was fighting in the streets.

Very few of the cities of Lywm-an-Esh were walled and Llarak was no exception. She had long, low houses of stone and carved timber, all brightly painted. The house of the Duke of Bedwilral was not immediately evident for it was little different from the other larger houses in the city, but Rhalina pointed it out. The fighting was quite close to the duke's residence and near it a building was burning.

The company of Allomglyl began to ride down towards the city, leaving the women in the hills.

"It seems some of those Chaos priests were more persuasive than Verenak," Prince Corum shouted to Rhalina as she prepared her spear.

They galloped into the outskirts of the town. The streets were empty and silent. From the centre came a great noise of battle.

"You had best lead us," he said to her, "for you'll know who are the duke's men and who are not."

She increased her speed without a word and they followed her into the middle of Llarak-an-Fol.

There they were. Men in blue livery with helmets and shields similar to those borne by Rhalina's men were fighting a mixed force of peasants and what were evidently professional soldiers.

"The men in blue are the duke's," she called. "Those in brown and purple are the city guard. There was always, I gather, a certain rivalry between the two."

Corum felt reluctance to engage them, not because he was afraid but because he bore no malice towards them.

The peasants, in particular, hardly knew why they fought and doubtless the city guard was barely conscious of the fact that Chaos was working through them to create conflict. They had been filled with a vague sense of unrest and, with the pushing of the priests of Urleh, had resorted to anger and to arms.

But Rhalina was already leading her horsemen through in a lance charge. The spears dipped and the cavalry drove into the mass of men, cutting a wide path through their ranks. Most of the enemy was unmounted and Corum's axe flew up and down as he chopped at the heads of those who, still with astonishment on their faces, sought to stop his advance. His horse reared and whinnied and its hoofs flailed and at least a dozen peasants and guards had died before they had joined with the duke's men and had turned to drive back the way they had come.

Already, to Corum's relief, many of the peasants had dropped their weapons and were running. The few guards fought on and now Corum could see armed priests fighting with them. A small man—almost a dwarf—on a big yellow charger, a massive broadsword in his left hand, was shouting encouragement to the newcomers. By his dress Corum decided that this must be the duke himself.

"Lay down your arms!" the small man yelled to the guards. "You will have mercy! You will be spared!"

Corum saw a guard look about him and then drop his

sword. Instantly the man was cut down by the Chaos priest nearest to him.

"Fight to the death!" screamed the priest. "If you betray Chaos now your souls will suffer more than your bodies could!"

But the surviving guards had plainly lost heart and one of them turned with resentment on the priest who had slain his comrade. His sword slashed at the man who went down trying to staunch the blood that suddenly erupted from his severed jugular.

Corum sheathed his war-axe. The pathetic little battle was virtually over. Rhalina's men and the warriors in blue livery closed on the few who still fought and disarmed them.

The small man on the large horse rode up to where Rhalina had joined Corum and Jhary-a-Conel. The little black-and-white cat still clung to Jhary's shoulder and it looked more puzzled than frightened by what it had witnessed.

"I am Duke Gwelhen of Bedwilral," announced the small man. "I thank thee mightily for thine aid. But I recognize thee not. Thou art not from Nyvish or Adwyn and, if ye be from farther afield, then ye could not have heard of my plight in time to save me!"

Rhalina removed her helm. She spoke as formally as the duke. "Dost thou not recognize me, Duke Gwelhen?"

"I fear not. My memory for faces…"

She laughed. "It was many years past. I am Rhalina who married your cousin's son…"

"Whose responsibility was the Margravate of Allomglyl. But I learned that he died in a shipwreck."

"It is so," she said gravely.

"But I thought Castle Moidel taken by the sea these many years. Where have you been in the meantime, my child?"

"Until recently I ruled at Moidel, but now the barbarians of the east have driven us out and we ride to warn you that what you have experienced here today is only a trifle of what Chaos will do if unchecked."

Duke Gwelhen rubbed at his beard. He returned his attention to the prisoners for a moment and issued some orders, then he smiled slowly. "Well, well. And who is this brave fellow with the eye-patch—and this one, who has a pretty cat on his shoulder, and..."

She laughed. "I will explain, Duke Gwelhen, if we may guest in your hall."

"I would hope that you would! Come. This sad business is done. We'll to the hall now."

In Gwelhen's simple hall they ate a meal of cheese and cold meats washed down by locally brewed beer.

"We are not used to fighting these days," Gwelhen said after introductions had been made and they had explained how they came to Llarak. "In some ways today's skirmish was a bloodier business than it might have been. If my men had more experience, they might have contained the thing and taken most of them prisoner, but they panicked. And it's likely that I'd have been dead by now if your company had not arrived. But all you tell me of this war between Law and Chaos makes sense of various moods I have had of late. You heard how I banished the Temple of Urleh? Its adherents had taken to morbid, unhealthy pursuits. There were some murders—other things... I could not explain them. We are content here. None starves or goes in need of anything. There was no reason for the unrest. So we are victims of powers beyond our control, are we? I like not that—whether it be Law or Chaos. I would prefer to remain neutral..."

"Aye," said Jhary-a-Conel. "Any thinking man does in these

conflicts. Yet there are times when sides must be taken lest all that one loves is destroyed. I have never known another answer to the problem, though the taking of an extreme position will always make a man lose something of his humanity."

"My feelings," murmured Gwelhen, motioning with his beer mug at Jhary.

"And all of ours," Rhalina agreed. "Yet unless we are ready for King Lyr's attack, Lywm-an-Esh will be brutally destroyed."

"She is dying, for the sea takes more land every year," said Gwelhen thoughtfully. "Yet she should die at her own speed. We must convince the king, however…"

"Who rules now in Halwyg-nan-Vake?" Rhalina asked.

He looked at her in surprise. "The Margravate was indeed remote! Onald-an-Gyss is our king. He is old Onald's nephew—his uncle died without issue…"

"And what of his temperament—for these things are decided on temperament—does he favour Law or Chaos?"

"Law, I would think, but I cannot say the same for his captains. Military men being what they are…"

"Perhaps they have already decided," Jhary murmured. "If the whole land is seized by the strife we have witnessed thus far, then a strong man supporting Chaos might have deposed the king, just as an attempt was made to depose you, Duke Gwelhen."

"We must ride at once to Halwyg," Corum said.

The duke nodded. "Aye—at once. Yet a largish company rides with you. It would be a week at least before you reached the capital."

"The company must follow us," Rhalina decided. "Beldan, will you command it and bring it to Halwyg?"

Beldan grimaced. "Aye, though I wish I could ride with you."

Corum got up from the table. "Then we three will set off for

Halwyg tonight. If we may rest an hour or two, Duke Gwelhen, we should be grateful."

Gwelhen's face was grave. "I would advise it. For all we know, you'll have little chance for much rest in the days to come."

THE WALL BETWEEN THE REALMS

Their riding was swift and it was across a land growing increasingly disturbed, with a people becoming more and more distressed without understanding why these moods descended on them or why they suddenly thought in terms of violence when a short time before they had thought only in terms of love.

And the priests of Chaos, many of them believing themselves to be acting from benevolent motives, continued to encourage strife and uncertainty.

They heard many rumours when they stopped to refresh themselves briefly or to change horses, but none of the rumours came close to the much more terrifying truth and soon they gave up their warnings until they should speak with the king himself so that he might then issue a decree which would carry his authority.

But would they convince the king? What evidence was there that they spoke the truth?

This was the great doubt in their minds as they rode for Halwyg-nan-Vake, across a beautiful landscape of soft hills and quiet farms which might soon be all destroyed.

Halwyg-nan-Vake was an old city of spires and pale stones. From all directions across the plain came white roads, leading to Halwyg. Along these roads travelled merchants and soldiers, peasants and priests, as well as the players and musicians in which Lywm-an-Esh was so rich. Down the Great East Way galloped Corum and Rhalina and Jhary, their armour and their clothes covered in dust, their eyes heavy with weariness.

Halwyg was a walled city, but the walls seemed more decorative than functional, their stonework carved with fanciful motifs, mythical beasts and complicated scenes of the city's past glories. None of the gates was closed as they came near and there were only a few sleepy guards who did not bother to hail them when they passed through and found themselves in streets filled with flowers. Every building had a garden surrounding it and every window had boxes in which more plants grew. The city was filled with the rich scents of the flowers and it seemed to Corum, remembering the Plain of Blossoms, that the main business of these people seemed to lie in the nurturing of lovely growing things.

And when they came to the palace of the king, they saw that every tower and battlement, every wall was covered in vines and flowers so that it seemed from a distance to be a castle built entirely of flowers. Even Corum smiled with pleasure when he saw it.

"It is magnificent," he said. "How could anyone wish to destroy all this?"

Jhary looked dubiously at the palace. "But they will," he said. "The barbarians will."

Rhalina addressed herself to a guard at the low wall.

"We come with news for King Onald," she said. "We have travelled far and swiftly and the news is urgent."

The guard, dressed in a handsome, but most unwarlike, fashion, saluted her. "I will see that the king is informed if you will kindly wait here."

And then, at last, they were escorted into the presence of the king.

He sat in a sunlit room which had a view over most of the southern part of the city. There were maps of his country upon a marble table and these had recently been consulted. He was young, with small features and a small frame which made him look almost like a boy. As they entered he rose gracefully to welcome them. He was dressed in a simple robe of pale yellow samite and there was a circlet upon his auburn hair which was the only indication of his station.

"You are tired," he said when he saw them. He signed to a servant. "Bring comfortable chairs and refreshment." He remained standing until the chairs had been brought and they were all seated near the window with a small table nearby on which food and wine were placed.

"I am told you come with urgent news," said King Onald. "Have you travelled from our eastern coasts?"

"From the west," said Corum.

"The *west*? Is trouble beginning there, also?"

"Excuse me, King Onald," Rhalina said, removing her helmet and shaking out her long hair, "but we were not aware that there was any strife in the east."

"Raiders," he said. "Barbarian pirates. Not long since they took the port of Dowish-an-Wod and razed it, slaying all. Several fleets, as far as we can gather, striking at different points along the coast. In most parts the citizens were unprepared and fell before they could begin to fight, but in one or two small towns the garrisons were able to resist the raiders and, in one case, took prisoners. One of those prisoners has recently been brought here. He is mad."

"Mad?" Jhary said.

"Aye—he believes himself to be some kind of crusader, destined to destroy the whole land of Lywm-an-Esh. He speaks of supernatural help, of an enormous army which marches against us…"

"He is not mad," Corum told him quietly. "At least, not in that respect. That is why we are here—to warn you of a huge invasion. The barbarians of Bro-an-Mabden—doubtless your coastal attackers—and the barbarians of the land you know as Bro-an-Vadhagh have united, called on the aid of Chaos and those creatures which serve Chaos, and are pledged to destroy all who side, knowingly or unknowingly, with the Lords of Law. For Lord Arioch of Chaos has been but lately banished from this particular domain of Five Planes and can only return if all who support Law are vanquished. His sister Queen Xiombarg cannot give aid directly, but she encourages all her servitors to throw their weight behind the barbarians."

King Onald stroked his lips with a thin finger. "It is graver than I had imagined. I was hard put to think of effective ways of stopping the coastal attacks, but now I can think of nothing which will enable us to resist such a force."

"Your people must be warned of their peril," said Rhalina urgently.

"Of course," replied the king. "We will reopen the arsenals and arm every man that we can. But even then…"

"You have forgotten how to fight?" suggested Jhary.

The king nodded. "You have read my thoughts, sir."

"If only Lord Arkyn had consolidated his power over this domain!" Corum said. "He could aid us. But now there is too little time. Lyr's army marches from the east and his allies sail from the north…"

"And doubtless this city is their ultimate destination," murmured Onald. "We cannot possibly withstand the might which you say they command."

"And we do not know what supernatural allies they have," Rhalina reminded him. "We could not remain any longer at Moidel to discover that." She explained how they had learned of Lyr's ambitions and Jhary smiled.

"I regret," he said, "that my little cat cannot fly over great stretches of water. The idea distresses him too much."

"Perhaps the priests of Law can help us…" Onald said thoughtfully.

"Perhaps," agreed Corum, "but I fear they have little power at this moment."

"And there are no allies we can call upon," Onald sighed. "Well, we must prepare to die."

The three fell silent.

A little later a servant entered and whispered something to the king. He looked surprised and turned to his guests.

"We are all four summoned to the Temple of Law," he said. "Perhaps the powers of the priests are greater than we know, for they seem aware of your presence in the city." To the servant he said, "Have a carriage prepared to take us there please."

While they waited for the carriage, they bathed quickly and cleaned their clothes as best they could and then the little party left the palace and entered the simple, open carriage which bore them through the streets until it came to a low, pleasant building on the western side of the city. A man stood at the entrance. He looked agitated. He was dressed in a long white robe on which was embroidered the single straight arrow which was the symbol of Law. He had a short grey beard, long grey hair and his skin was also almost grey. In all this, his large brown eyes seemed to belong to another.

He bowed as the king approached.

"Greetings, my lord king. Greetings, Lady Rhalina, Prince Corum and Sir Jhary-a-Conel. Forgive me for the sudden nature of my summons but—but..." He made a vague gesture and then led them into the cool temple which was almost entirely undecorated.

"I am Aleryon-a-Nyvish," said the priest. "I was awakened early this morning by—by—my master's master. He told me many things, but ended by naming the names of you three travelers and saying that you would soon be at the Court of the king. He said I must bring you here..."

"Your master's master?" Corum said.

"The Lord Arkyn himself. The Lord Arkyn, Prince Corum. None other."

And then, from the shadows at the far end of the hall a tall man walked. He was a comely man, dressed like a nobleman of Lywm-an-Esh. There was a gentle smile upon his face and his eyes seemed full of a sad wisdom.

The form had changed, but Corum immediately recognized the presence as that of Arkyn of Law.

"My lord Arkyn," he said.

"Good Corum, how dost thou fare?"

"My mind is full of fear," Corum replied. "For Chaos comes against us all."

"I know, but it will be long before I can rid my domain of Arioch's entire influence—just as it took him a great long time to rid the domain of mine. There is little material aid I can offer thee as yet, for I am still gathering my strength. However, there are other ways in which I can help. I can tell you that Lyr's allies have now joined him and that they are dreadful things from the nether regions. I can tell you that Lyr has another ally—an unhuman sorcerer who is the personal messenger of Queen Xiombarg and is capable of summoning further aid from her plane, though she would destroy herself if she attempted to come into this realm in person."

"But where might *we* find allies, Lord Arkyn?" Jhary asked reasonably.

"Do you not know, you of many names?" smiled Lord Arkyn. He had recognized Jhary-a-Conel for what he was.

"I know that if there be an answer then it may well be some form of paradox," Jhary replied. "That is one thing I have learned in my profession as companion to champions."

Again Arkyn smiled. "Existence is a paradox, friend Jhary. Everything that is Good is also Evil. You know that, I am sure."

"Aye. That is what makes me so insouciant."

"And it is what makes you so concerned?"

"Aye." Jhary laughed. "Then is there an answer, my Lord of Law?"

"That is why I am here, to tell you that unless you find aid for yourselves then Lywm-an-Esh will of a certainty perish and with it the cause of Law. You know that you have not the strength, ferocity or experience to withstand Lyr, Glandyth and the rest—particularly since they may now call upon the power of the Dog and the Bear. There is one people of whom I know who may be willing to ally themselves with your cause. But they do not exist in this plane—or in any of the planes I rule. Save for yourself, Corum, Arioch had succeeded in destroying all with the power to resist Chaos."

"Where do they exist, my lord?" Corum asked.

"In the Realm of Queen Xiombarg of Chaos."

"She must be our bitterest enemy!" Rhalina gasped. "If we could enter her realm—and I do not see how that is possible—she would welcome the chance to slay us!"

"I know that she would—once she found you," Lord Arkyn agreed. "But if you went to her realm you would have to hope that her attention would be so focused on the events in this realm that she would not realize you had entered her own."

"And what is there that might help us?" Jhary said. "Surely nothing of Law! Queen Xiombarg was more powerful then her brother Arioch. Chaos must hold full sway in her realm."

"Not quite—and not so much as in her brother Mabelode's realm... There is a city in her realm which has resisted all she could have brought against it. It is called the City in the Pyramid and the people who dwell in it are of a highly sophisticated civilization. If you can reach the City in the Pyramid, you may find the allies you need."

"But how can we travel to Xiombarg's realm?" Corum said reasonably. "We have no such powers."

"I can make it possible for you to do that."

"And how, in five planes, shall we find a single city?" Jhary asked.

"You must ask," said Arkyn simply. "Ask for the City in the Pyramid. The city which has resisted Xiombarg's attacks. Will you go? It is all that I can suggest if you would be saved..."

"And if you, too, are to be saved," Jhary pointed out with a smile. "I know you gods and I know that you manipulate mortals only to achieve those things you cannot yourselves achieve, for mortals may scurry where gods may not go. Have you other motives in encouraging this course of action, Lord Arkyn?"

Lord Arkyn looked humorously at Jhary. "You know the ways of gods, as you say. But I can tell you no more save that I gamble with your lives as freely as I gamble with my own destiny. What you risk, I risk. If you do not succeed in all I hope, then I will perish, all that is gentle and good in this realm will perish. And you need not go to Xiombarg's realm..."

"If there are potential allies there, then we will go," Corum said firmly.

"Then I will open the Wall Between the Realms," said Arkyn quietly.

He turned and walked back into the shadows.

"Ready yourselves," he said. He was now invisible.

Corum heard a sound in his head—a sound that was soundless, but which blocked out all other sounds. He looked at the others. They were evidently experiencing the same thing. Something moved in front of his eyes—a dim pattern superimposed on the more solid scene which showed his companions and the simple walls of the temple. Something vibrated.

And then it was there.

A cruciform shape stood in the middle of the temple. They moved around it in wonder but, from whatever angle they regarded it, it retained the same perspective. It was a shimmering silver in the cool darkness of the temple and through it, as through a window, they could see part of a landscape.

Arkyn's voice came from behind them.

"There is the entrance to Xiombarg's domain."

Strange black birds flew across the section of sky they could observe through the peculiar window. A distant sound of cackling.

Corum shivered. Rhalina moved closer to him.

Now King Onald's voice: "If you would stay here, I will think no less of you…"

"We must go," Corum said almost dreamily. "We must."

But Jhary, with a suggestion of defiant jauntiness, was the first to step through and stand there, looking up at the unpleasant birds, stroking his cat.

"How shall we return?" Corum said.

"If you are successful, then you will find the means to return," said Arkyn. His voice was growing weaker. "Hurry. It takes much from me to hold the gateway open."

Hand in hand with Rhalina, Corum stepped through and looked back.

The cruciform shape of shimmering silver was fading. They saw Onald's concerned face for an instant and then it was gone.

"So this is Xiombarg's realm," said Jhary with a sniff. "It has a brooding air about it."

Black mountains lay on two sides and the sky was bleak. The horrid birds flew into the mountains, still screaming. Ahead, a foul sea washed a rocky shore.

BOOK TWO

IN WHICH PRINCE CORUM AND HIS
COMPANIONS GAIN THE FURTHER
ENMITY OF CHAOS AND EXPERIENCE
A STRANGE, NEW FORM OF SORCERY

THE LAKE OF VOICES

"WHICH WAY?" JHARY looked about him. "The sea or the mountains? Neither's inviting…"

Corum sighed deeply. The morbid landscape had instantly depressed him. Rhalina touched his arm, her eyes full of sympathy.

Though she looked at Corum, she spoke to Jhary who was now adjusting his ever-present sack on his shoulder. "Inland would be best, surely, since we have no boat."

"And no horses," Jhary reminded her. "It will be a fearful long walk. And who's to say those mountains are passable when we reach 'em?"

Corum gave Rhalina a quick, sad smile of gratitude. He straightened his shoulders. "Well, we made up our minds to enter this realm, now we must make up our minds which way to go." His hand on the pommel of his sword, he stared towards the mountains. "I have seen something of the power of Chaos when I journeyed to Arioch's Court, but it seems to me that that power extends further in this realm. We'll head towards the mountains. There we may discover some inhabitants who may know where lies this City in the Pyramid Lord Arkyn mentioned."

And they set off over the unpleasantly mottled rock.

A while later it became evident that the sun had not moved across the sky. The brooding silence continued, broken only by the ghastly screechings of the black birds which nested in the peaks of the mountains. It was a land which seemed to radiate despair. For a short time Jhary had attempted to whistle a bright little tune, but the sound had died, as if swallowed by the desolate land.

"I thought Chaos all howling, random creativity," said Corum. "This is worse."

"It is what becomes of a place when Chaos exhausts its invention," Jhary told him. "Ultimately, Chaos brings a more profound stagnation than anything it despises in Law. It must forever seek more and more sensation, more and more empty marvels, until there is nothing left and it has forgotten what true invention is."

And at length weariness overcame them and they lay down on the barren rock and slept. When they awoke it was to observe that only one thing had changed…

The great black birds were closer. They were wheeling overhead in the sky.

"What can they live on?" Rhalina wondered. "There is no game here, no vegetation. Where is their food?"

Jhary looked significantly at Corum who shrugged.

"Come," said the Prince in the Scarlet Robe. "Let's continue.

Time may be relative, but I have a feeling that unless we accomplish our mission soon, Lywm-an-Esh will fall."

And the birds circled lower so that they could see their leathery wings and bodies, their tiny, greedy eyes, their long vicious beaks.

A small, fierce sound escaped from the throat of Jhary's cat. It arched its back slightly as it glared at the birds.

They trudged on until the ground began to rise more sharply and they had reached the nearer slopes of the mountains.

The mountains squatted over them like sleeping monsters that might at any moment awake and devour them. The rocks were glassy, slippery and they climbed them slowly.

Still the black birds wheeled among the crags and now they were certain that if they allowed themselves to sleep the birds would descend and attack. This knowledge alone kept them climbing.

The frightful screeching grew louder, more insistent, almost gleeful. They heard the flap of obscene wings over their heads, but they refused to look up, as this would have wasted a fraction of the energy they had left.

They were looking now for shelter, for a crack in the rock into which they might crawl and defend themselves against the birds when, finally, they attacked.

They could hear the sound of their own gasping breath, the scrape of their feet on the stone, mingling with the flappings and screechings of the black birds.

Corum spared a glance for Rhalina and saw that there was desperate fear in her eyes and that she was weeping as she climbed. He began to feel that he had been tricked by Arkyn, that they had been sent, cynically, to their doom in this wasteland.

Then the flapping filled his ears and he felt the slap of cold air against his face and a talon grazed his helmet. With a strangled

Gloucester Library
P.O. Box 2380
Gloucester, VA 23061

cry he felt for his sword and tried to tug it from the scabbard. He looked up in terror and saw a mass of black, flapping, savage things with glaring eyes and snapping beaks. The sword came free and, wearily, he lunged out at the birds. They cackled sardonically as his sword failed to find flesh. Suddenly his six-fingered jeweled hand reached out instead, moving without his volition, and it clutched one of the birds by its scrawny throat and squeezed that throat as it had squeezed human throats before. The bird gave a single surprised squawk and died. The Hand of Kwll threw the corpse to the glassy rock. The birds flapped a little distance away in consternation and settled in the nearby crags watching Corum warily. It had been so long since the hand had acted in that way that Corum had almost forgotten its powers. For the first time since it had destroyed the Heart of Arioch he was grateful to it. He displayed it to the birds and they made disturbed sounds in their throats, eyeing the corpse of their dead companion.

Rhalina, who had not witnessed the power of the Hand of Kwll before, looked with relieved astonishment at Corum. But Jhary merely pursed his lips and took advantage of the pause to draw his sword and lay propped on his elbows against the hard rock, his cat still on his shoulder.

And thus they sat, the birds and the human beings, regarding each other beneath the silent, brooding sky on the slopes of the bleak mountains, until it occurred to Corum that if the Hand of Kwll had saved them from their immediate danger, the Eye of Rhynn might prove even more useful. But he was reluctant to raise the eye-patch and look with the eye's full powers into that strange nether region from which he could sometimes summon ghostly allies—the dead men earlier slain at his command. And, particularly, he did not want to summon those last who had been slain at the command of the Hand and the Eye—Queen Oorese's subjects, the Vadhagh riders, his own race, who had been slain by accident. But something must be done to break this impasse, for none of them had the strength to resist a mass attack by the birds and even if the Hand of Kwll should slay one or two more it would not save Rhalina and Jhary-a-Conel. Reluctantly his hand began to rise towards the jeweled eye-patch.

And then the patch was off and the horrid, faceted, alien eye of the dead god Rhynn glared into a world even more dreadful than the one they presently inhabited.

Again Corum saw a cavern in which dim shapes moved hopelessly this way and that. And in the foreground were the beings he had least wished to see. Their dead eyes peered out at him and there was a frightening sadness about the set of their faces. They had wounds in their bodies, but the wounds did not bleed, for these were now the creatures of limbo, neither dead nor alive. Their mounts were with them, too—creatures with thick, scaly bodies, cloven feet and nests of horns jutting from their snouts. The last of the Vadhagh folk—a lost part of the race which had once inhabited the Flamelands created by Arioch for his amusement. They were dressed from head to foot in red, tight-fitting garments, with red hoods on their heads. In their hands were their long, barbed lances.

Corum could not bear to look upon them and he made to move the eye-patch back into place, but then the Hand of Kwll had reached out, reached into that frightful limbo, and was gesturing to the dead Vadhagh. Slowly the score of corpses moved forward in answer to the summons. Slowly they mounted their horned beasts. Slowly they rode out of that ghastly cavern in a nameless netherworld and stood, a company of death, upon the slippery slopes of the mountains.

The birds screeched in surprise and anger but for some reason they did not take to the air. They shifted from foot to foot and darted their beaks at the scarlet warriors who now advanced upon them.

The black birds waited until the dead Vadhagh were almost upon them before they began to flap their wings and fly skyward.

Rhalina was staring in horror at the scene. "By all the Great Old Gods, Corum—what new foulness is this?"

"It is a foulness which aids us," said Corum grimly. And he called out, "Strike!"

And the barbed lances were flung by scarlet arms and found the heads of each black bird. There was an agitation in the air and then the creatures had fallen to the slopes.

Rhalina continued to watch wide-eyed as the living-dead riders dismounted and went to collect their prizes. Corum had learned what happened in that netherworld whenever he summoned aid from it. By calling upon his earlier victims he could have their aid if he supplied them with victims of their own—then these victims would replace them and presumably the souls of the first victims would be released to find peace. He hoped that this was so.

The leading Vadhagh picked up two of the birds by their throats and slung them over his back. He turned a face that was half shorn away and looked through eyeless sockets at Corum.

"It is done, master," droned the dead voice.

"Then you may return," said Corum, half-choking.

"Before I go, I must impart a message to you, master."

"A message? From whom?"

"From One Who is Closer to You than You Know," said the dead Vadhagh mechanically. "He says that you must seek the Lake of Voices, that if you have the courage to sail across it then you might find help in your quest."

"The Lake of Voices. Where is it? Who is this creature you speak of…"

"The Lake of Voices lies beyond this mountain range. Now I depart, master. We thank you for our prizes."

Corum could bear no longer to look at the Vadhagh. He turned away, replacing the jeweled patch over his eye. When he looked back the Vadhagh had gone and so had the birds, all save the one which had been slain by the Hand of Kwll.

Rhalina's face was pale. "These 'allies' of yours are no better than creatures of Chaos! It must corrupt us to use them, Corum…"

Jhary got up from the position in which he had been before the arrival of Corum's ghastly warriors. "It is Chaos which corrupts us," he said lightly, "which makes us fight. Chaos brutalizes all—even those who do not serve it. That you must accept, Lady Rhalina. I know it is the truth."

She lowered her eyes. "Let us make our way to this lake," she said. "What was its name?"

"A strange one." Corum looked back at the last dead bird. "The Lake of Voices."

They trudged on through the mountains, resting frequently now that the danger of the birds had been removed, beginning to feel a new threat—that of hunger and thirst, for they had no provisions with them.

Eventually they began to descend and they saw sparse grass growing on the lower slopes and beyond the grass a lake of blue water—a calm and beautiful lake which they could not believe existed in any realm of Chaos.

"It is lovely!" Rhalina gasped. "And we might find food there— and at least we shall be able to quench our thirst."

"Aye…" said Corum, more suspiciously.

And Jhary said, "I think your informant said we should need courage to cross it. I wonder what danger it holds."

They could barely walk by the time they reached the grassy slopes and left the harsh rock behind them. On the grass they rested and they found a spring nearby so that they did not have to wait until they reached the lake to quench their thirst. Jhary murmured a word to his cat which sprang suddenly into the air on its wings and was soon lost from sight.

"Where have you sent the cat, Jhary?" asked Corum.

Jhary winked at him. "Hunting," he said.

Sure enough, in a very short time the cat returned with a small rabbit, almost as big as itself, in its claws. It deposited the rabbit and then left to find another. Jhary busied himself with the building of a fire and soon they had feasted and were sleeping while one of their number kept watch until he was relieved by another.

Then they continued on their way until they were less than a quarter of a mile from the shores of the lake.

It was then that Corum paused, cocking his head on one side.

"Do you hear them?" he asked.

"I hear nothing," Rhalina said.

But Jhary nodded. "Aye—voices—as of a great throng heard in the distance. Voices…"

"That is what I hear," Corum agreed.

And as they neared the lake, walking swiftly over the springy turf, the babble of voices increased until it filled their heads and they covered their ears in horror for they realized now why it would take courage to cross the Lake of Voices.

The words—the murmurings, the pleadings, the oaths, the shouts, the crying, the laughter—they were all issuing from the blue waters of the apparently peaceful lake.

It was the water that spoke.

It was as if a million people had been drowned in it and continued to talk although their bodies had rotted and been dispersed by the liquid.

Looking desperately about him, his hands still covering his ears, Corum saw that it would be impossible to try to skirt the Lake of Voices for it was apparent that on both sides of them there stretched marshland which they would be unable to cross.

He forced himself to move closer to the water and the voices of the men and the women and the children were like the voices which must populate hell.

"Please..."

"I wish—I wish—I wish..."

"Nobody will..."

"This agony..."

"There is no peace..."

"Why...?"

"It was a lie. I was deceived..."

"I, too, was deceived. I cannot..."

"Aaaaaaa! Aaaaaaa! Aaaaaaa!"

"Help me, I beg thee..."

"Help me!"

"Me!"

"The fate which cannot be borne except with..."

"Ha!"

"Help..."

"Be merciful..."

"Save her—save her—save her..."

"*I suffer so much...*"

"*Ha, ha, ha, ha, ha, ha, ha, ha, ha, ha, ha, ha, ha, ha, ha, ha, ha, ha, ha, ha, ha, ha, ha, ha...*"

"*It seemed so splendid and there were lights all around...*"

"*Beasts, beasts, beasts, beasts, beasts...*"

"*The child... It was the child...*"

"*All morning it wept until the lurching thing entered me...*"

"*Soweth! Tebel art...*"

"*Forlorn in Rendane I composed that strain...*"

"*Peace...*"

And then Corum saw that a boat was waiting for them on the shore of the Lake of Voices.

And he wondered if he would be sane by the time they reached the other side.

2

THE WHITE RIVER

ORUM AND JHARY hauled on the boat's long oars while Rhalina lay sobbing in the bow. With every pull upon the oars the water was disturbed further and instead of a splashing sound a new babble of voices broke out. They sensed that the voices did not come from beneath the water but from within it—as if every single drop of water contained a human soul which expressed its pain and the terror of its situation. Corum could not help but wonder if every lake in existence were not like this and that this was the only one they could actually hear. He strove to shut his mind to such fearful speculation.

"*Wish that...*"

"*Would that...*"

"*If I...*"

"*Could I...*"

"*Love—love—love...*"

"*Sad soothing songs seeking souls so soft so sensitive seeming smooth silken...*"

"Stop! Stop!" begged Rhalina, but the voices went on and Corum and Jhary pulled the harder on their oars, their lips moving in pain.

"*I wish—I wish—I wish—I wish...*"

"*Curl awake in kitten time the condemnation of my...*"

"*Once—once—once...*"

"*Help us!*"

"*Release us!*"

"*Give us peace! Peace!*"

"*Please, peace, please, peace...*"

"*Opening without resort...*"

"*Cold...*"

"*Cold...*"

"*Cold...*"

"We cannot help you!" Corum groaned. "There is nothing we can do!"

Rhalina was screaming now.

Only Jhary-a-Conel kept his lips tight shut, his eyes fixed on the middle distance, his body moving rhythmically back and forth as he continued to row.

"*Oh, save us!*"

"*Save me!*"

"*The child is—the child...*"

"*Bad, mad, sad, glad, bad, sad, mad, glad, mad, bad, glad, sad...*"

"Be silent! We can do nothing!"

"Corum! Corum! Stop them! Is there no sorcery at your command which will hush their voices?"

"None."

"*Aaaah!*"

"*Oorum canish, oorum canish, oorum canish, sashan faroom*

alann alann, oorum canish, oorum canish..."

"*Ha, ha, ha, ha, ha, ha...*"

"*Nobody, nothing, nowhere, needless misery, what purpose doth it serve, which man benefits?*"

"*Whisper softly, whisper low, whisper, whisper...*"

"*No, no, no, no, no, no, no, no, no, no, no...*"

Now Corum released one hand from his oar and slapped at his head as if trying to drive the voices out. Rhalina had collapsed completely on the bottom of the boat and he could not distinguish her cries, her pleadings and demands, from the others.

"Stop!"

"*Stop, stop, stop, stop...*"

"*Stop...*"

"*Stop...*"

"*Stop...*"

There were tears flowing down Jhary's face, but he rowed on, not once altering the rhythm of his movements. Only the cat seemed undisturbed. It sat on the seat between him and Corum and it washed its paws. To the cat the water was like any other water and thus to be avoided as much as possible. Once or twice it cast nervous glances over the side of the boat but that was all.

"*Save us, save us, save us...*"

Then a deeper voice, a warm, humorous, pleasant voice, cut through the others and it said:

"*Why do you not join them? It would save you this misery. All you need do is to stop your rowing and leave the boat and enter the water and relax, becoming one with the rest. Why be proud?*"

"No! Do not listen! Listen to me!"

"*Listen to us!*"

"*Listen to me!*"

"*Do not listen to them. They are really happy. It is just that your coming disturbs them. They wish you to join them—to join them—to join them—to join them...*"

"*No, no, no!*"

"No!" screamed Corum. He plucked the oar from the rowlocks and he began to beat at the waters of the lake. "Stop! Stop! Stop!"

"Corum!" Jhary spoke for the first time. He clung to the side as the boat rocked badly from side to side. Rhalina looked up in terror.

"Corum! You will make it worse. You will destroy us if we fall into the lake!" Jhary cried.

"Stop! Stop! Stop!"

Keeping one arm on his own oar Jhary reached across and tugged at Corum's scarlet robe. "Corum! Desist!"

Corum sat down suddenly and looked strangely at Jhary as if he were an enemy. Then his expression softened and he put the oar back in its place and began to row. The shore was not too distant now.

"We must get to the shore," Jhary said. "It is the only way in which we'll escape the voices. You must hang on a little longer, that is all."

"Yes," said Corum. "Yes..." And he resumed his rowing and avoided looking at Rhalina's tortured features.

"*Molten sleeping snakes and old owls and hungry hawks populate my memories of Charatatu...*"

"*Join them and all the splendid memories may be shared. Join them, Prince Corum, Lady Rhalina, Sir Jhary. Join them. Join them. Join them.*"

"Who are you?" Corum said. "Did you do this to them all?"

"*I am the Voice of the Lake of Voices, that is all. I am the true spirit of the Lake. I offer peace and union with all your fellow souls. Do not listen to the minority of discontented ones. They would be discontented wherever they were. There are always such spirits…"*

"No, no, no, no…"

And Corum and Jhary pulled even harder on their sweeps until suddenly the boat scraped up the shore and there was an angry motion in the water and a huge water spout suddenly appeared and began to whine and roar and scream and shout.

"NO! I WILL NOT BE THWARTED! YOU ARE MINE! NONE ESCAPES THE LAKE OF VOICES!"

The water spout assumed a form and they could see a fierce, writhing face there—a face full of rage. Hands, too, formed from the water and began to reach out for them.

"YOU ARE MINE! YOU WILL SING WITH THE REST! YOU WILL BE PART OF MY CHORUS!"

The three scrambled hastily from the boat and dashed up the shore with the water thing growing larger and larger behind them and its voice roaring louder and louder.

"YOU ARE MINE! YOU ARE MINE! I WILL NOT ALLOW YOU TO GO!"

But a thousand tinier voices all babbled:

"Run—run swiftly—never return—run—run—run…"

"TRAITORS! STOP!"

And the voices stopped and there was silence until the roaring creature of water bellowed once more.

"NO! YOU HAVE MADE ME DISPEL THE VOICES—MY VOICES—MY PETS! I MUST BEGIN AFRESH TO COLLECT MY CHOIR! YOU HAVE MADE ME BANISH THEM! COME BACK! COME BACK!"

And the creature grew even taller as they ran all the faster, its watery hands reaching out for them.

Then, suddenly, with a scream, it began to tumble back into the lake, no longer able to sustain its shape. They watched it fall, they watched it writhe and gesticulate in anger and then it was gone and the lake was the peaceful stretch of blue water they had first seen.

But this time there were no voices. The souls were still. By accident the three had made the creature tell its captives to be silent and had evidently broken the spell which it had had over them.

Corum sighed and sat down on the grass. "It is over," he said. "And all those poor spirits are at rest now..."

He smiled at the expression of panic on the cat's face and he realized how much more horrifying their last experience had been to the little animal.

Then, when they had rested, they climbed the hill and looked down upon a desert.

It was a brown desert and through it ran a river. But it seemed that the river was not of water. It was white, like pure milk, and it was wide and it wandered lazily through the brown landscape.

Corum sighed. "It seems to go on for ever."

"Look," said Rhalina and she pointed. "Look, a rider!"

Mounting the brow of a hill and coming towards them was a man on a horse. He was slumped in the saddle and plainly had not seen them, but Corum drew his sword nonetheless, and the others drew theirs. The horse moved slowly, plodding on as if it had been walking for days.

They saw that the rider, dressed in patched and battered leather, was asleep in his saddle, a broadsword hanging by a thong from his right wrist, his left hand gripping the reins of the horse. He had a haggard face which gave no indication of his age, a great hooked nose and untrimmed hair and beard. He seemed a poor man, yet hanging on his saddle pommel was a crown which, though coated with dust, was plainly of gold studded with many precious gems.

"Is he a thief?" Rhalina wondered. "Has he stolen that crown and is trying to escape those who own it?"

When it was a few feet from them the horse stopped suddenly and looked at them with large, weary eyes. Then it bent and began to crop the grass.

At this the rider stirred. He opened his eyes. He rubbed them. He, too, peered at them and then seemed to ignore them. He mumbled to himself.

"Greetings, sir," said Corum.

The gaunt man screwed up his eyes and looked at Corum again. He reached down behind him for a water bottle, unstopped it and flung back his head to drink deeply. Then, deliberately, he put the stopper back into the bottle and replaced the thing behind him.

"Greetings," said Corum again.

The mounted man nodded at him. "Aye," he said.

"From where do you travel, sir?" Jhary asked. "We ourselves are lost and would appreciate some indication of what, for instance, lies beyond that brown waste there…"

The man sighed and looked at the waste, at the white, winding river.

"That is the Blood Plain," he said. "The river is called the White River—or by some the Milk River, though it is not milk…"

"Why the Blood Plain?" Rhalina asked.

The man stretched and frowned. "Because, madam, it is a plain and it is covered in blood. That brown dust is dried blood—blood spilled an age since in some forgotten battle between Law and Chaos, I understand."

"And what lies beyond it?" Corum said.

"Many things—none that is pleasant. Nothing is pleasant in this world since Chaos conquered it."

"You are not on the side of Chaos?"

"Why should I be? Chaos dispossessed me. Chaos exiled me. Chaos would have me dead, but I move all the while and have not been found yet. One day, perhaps…"

Jhary introduced his friends and then himself. "We seek a place called the City in the Pyramid," he told the haggard rider.

The rider laughed. "As do I. But I cannot believe it exists! I think Chaos pretends such a place resists it to offer hope to its enemies so that it may give them still more pain. I am called, sir, the King Without a Country. Noreg-Dan was once my name and I ruled a fair land and, I think, I ruled it wisely. But Chaos came and Chaos minions destroyed my nation and my subjects and left me alive to wander the world seeking a mythical city…"

"So you have no faith in the City in the Pyramid?"

"I have not found it thus far."

"Could it lie beyond the Blood Plain?" Corum asked.

"It could, but I'm not fool enough to cross it for it could be endless and you, on foot, would have a smaller chance than would I. I am not without courage," said King Noreg-Dan, "but I still retain a little common sense. If there was wood in these parts, perhaps it would be possible to build a boat and hope to cross the desert by means of the White River, but there is no wood…"

"But there is a boat," said Jhary-a-Conel.

"Would it be wise to go back to the Lake of Voices?" Rhalina cautioned.

"The Lake of Voices!" King Noreg-Dan shook his tangled head. "Do not go there—the voices will draw you in…"

Corum explained what had happened and the King Without a Country listened intently. Then he smiled and it was a smile of admiration. He dismounted from his horse and came close to Corum, inspecting him. "You're a strange-looking creature, sir, with your hand and your eye-patch and your odd armour, but you are a hero and I congratulate you—all of you." He addressed the others. "I'd say it would be worth a foray down to the beach and recover old Freenshak's boat—we could use my horse to haul it up here!"

"Freenshak?" Jhary said.

"One of the names of the creature you encountered. A particularly powerful water sprite which came when Xiombarg began her reign. Shall we try to get the boat?"

"Aye," grinned Corum. "We'll try."

Somewhat nervously they returned to the lake shore, but it seemed that Freenshak was beaten for the moment and they had no difficulty in harnessing the tired horse to the boat and pulling it up the hill and halfway down the other side. In a locker Corum found a sail and saw that a short mast was stowed in lugs along one side of the boat.

As they prepared the boat he said to King Noreg-Dan, "But what of your horse? There'll not be room…"

Noreg-Dan drew a deep breath. "It will be a shame, but I will have to abandon him. I think he will be safer alone than with me and, besides, he deserves a rest, for he has served me faithfully since I was forced to flee my land."

Noreg-Dan stripped the horse of his harness and put it in the boat. Then they began the hard task of dragging the vessel down the hill and across the brown, choking dust (all the more unpleasant now that they knew what the dust was) until they reached the nearest shore of the White River. The horse stood watching them from the hillside and then it turned away. Noreg-Dan lowered his head and folded his arms.

And still the sun had not moved across the sky and they had no means of knowing how much time had passed.

The liquid of the river was thicker than water and Noreg-Dan advised them not to touch it.

"It can have a corrosive effect on the skin," he said.

"But what is the stuff?" Rhalina asked as they pushed off and raised the sail. "Will it not rot the boat if it will rot our skin?"

"Aye," said the King Without a Country. "Eventually. We must hope we cross the desert before that happens." He looked back once more to where he had left his horse, but the horse had disappeared. "Some say that while the dust is the dried blood of mortals, the White River is the blood of the Great Old Gods which was spilled in the battle and which will not dry."

Rhalina pointed to the hillside from which the river appeared. "But that cannot be—it comes from somewhere and it goes somewhere…"

"Apparently," said Noreg-Dan.

"Apparently?"

"This land is ruled by Chaos," he reminded her.

A light breeze was blowing now and Corum raised the sail. The boat began to move more quickly and soon the hills were out of sight and there was nothing to be seen but the Blood Plain stretching to every horizon.

Rhalina slept for a long while and, in turns, the others slept also, there being little else to do. But when Rhalina awoke for the third time and still saw the Blood Plain, she murmured to herself: "So *much* blood spilled. So *much*…"

And still the boat sailed on down the milk-white river while Noreg-Dan told them something of what Xiombarg's reign had brought to this domain.

"All creatures not loyal to Chaos were destroyed or else,

like me, had jokes played upon them—the Sword Rulers are notorious for their jokes. Every degenerate and vicious impulse in mortals was let loose and horror fell upon this world. My wife, my children were…" He broke off. "All of us suffered. But whether this took place a year ago or a hundred, I know not, for it was part of Xiombarg's joke to stop the sun so that we should not know how much time passed…"

"If Xiombarg's rule began at the same time as Arioch's," Corum said, "then it was much more than one century, King Noreg-Dan…"

"Xiombarg appears to have abolished time on this plane," Jhary put in. "Relatively speaking, of course. What happened here happened at whatever time people agree upon…"

"As you say," Corum nodded. "But tell us what you have heard of the City in the Pyramid, King Noreg-Dan."

"It was not originally of this plane at all, I gather—though it existed on one of the Five Planes now ruled by Xiombarg. In its seeking to escape Chaos, it moved from one plane to another, but eventually it was forced to stop and merely be content with protecting itself against Queen Xiombarg's attacks. She has spent, I hear, much of her energy on those attacks. Perhaps that is why I and the few like me are still allowed to exist. I do not know."

"There are others?"

"Aye, other wanderers such as myself. Or, at least, there were. Perhaps Xiombarg has found them now…"

"Or perhaps they found the City in the Pyramid."

"Possibly."

"Xiombarg concentrates on watching events in the next realm," Jhary said knowledgeably. "She wants to see the outcome of the battle between the Chaos minions and those who serve Law."

"Just as well for you, Prince Corum," said Noreg-Dan. "For

if she knew the destroyer of her brother was actually where she could destroy him herself…"

"We'll not speak of that," said Corum.

On and on went the White River and they began to think that perhaps it and the Blood Plain were, indeed, without end, as this world was without time.

"Is there a name for the City in the Pyramid?" Jhary asked.

"You think it might be your Tanelorn?" Rhalina said.

He grinned and shook his head. "No. I know Tanelorn and that description would not, I think, fit it."

"Some say it is built within a huge, featureless pyramid," Noreg-Dan told him. "Others say it is merely a pyramid shape, like a great ziggurat. There are many myths, I fear, concerning the city."

"I do not think I have encountered such a city on my travels," Jhary said.

"It sounds to me," said Corum, "as if it resembles one of the great Sky Cities, such as the one which crashed over the Plain of Broggfythus during the last great battle between the Vadhagh and the Nhadragh. They exist in our legends and I know that one, at least, was real, for the wreckage used to be near Castle Erorn where I was born. Both Vadhagh and Nhadragh had these cities, which were capable of moving through the planes. But when that phase of our history was over, they disappeared and we began to live more contentedly in our castles…" He stopped himself from continuing that theme, for it only brought back the bitterness. "It might be such a city," he said rather lamely.

"I think we had better land this craft," said Jhary cheerfully.

"Why?" Corum's back was to the prow.

"Because the White River and the Blood Plain seem to have ended."

Corum looked and was instantly alert. They were heading for a cliff. The plain ended as if sliced off by a gigantic knife and the liquid of the White River was hurtling into the abyss.

3

BEASTS OF THE ABYSS

Now the White River foamed wildly and roared as it rushed over the brink. Corum and Jhary dragged the oars free and used them to steer the rocking boat towards the bank.

"Be ready to jump, Rhalina!" Corum yelled.

She stood upright, holding on to the mast. King Noreg-Dan steadied her.

The boat danced out into midstream again and then, as suddenly, swerved back towards the bank as another current caught it. Corum staggered and almost fell overboard as he manipulated the oar. The sound of the torrent almost drowned their voices. The abyss was much closer and it would not be much longer before they were all hurled over it. Dimly, through the spray, Corum saw the distant wall of the far cliff. It must have been a mile away at least.

Then the boat scraped the bank and Corum yelled, "Jump, Rhalina!"

And she jumped with Noreg-Dan leaping after her, his arms waving. She landed in the blood-dust and fell, sprawling.

Jhary jumped next. But the boat was turning out into the centre of the river again. He landed in the shallows and struggled towards the bank, shouting at Corum.

Corum remembered Noreg-Dan's warning about the properties of the white liquid, but there was nothing for it but to leap in, his mouth tight shut, and flounder for the bank, his armour dragging him down.

But the weight of the armour fought the current and his feet touched the bottom. Shuddering he climbed to the land, white droplets of liquid oozing down his body.

He lay panting on the bank and watched as the boat reared on the edge of the abyss and then fell from sight.

They staggered away from the White River, following the edge of the gorge, ankle-deep in the brown dust, and when the roar of the torrent had grown fainter they paused and tried to assess their situation.

The abyss seemed endless. It stretched to both horizons, its edges straight and its sides sheer. It was plain that it had not been created naturally. It was as if some gigantic canal had been planned to flow between the cliffs—a mile-wide canal, a mile deep.

They stood on the brink and looked down into the abyss. Corum felt vertigo seize him and he took a step backwards. The sides of the cliff were of the same dark obsidian as the mountains they had left earlier, but these sides were utterly smooth. Far, far below a yellowish vapour writhed, obscuring the bottom—if any bottom there were. The four people felt completely dwarfed by the vastness of the scene. They looked backwards across the Blood Plain. It was featureless, endless. They tried to make out details of the opposite cliff, but it was too distant.

A faint mist obscured the sun which still stood at noon above them.

The little figures began to tramp along the edge, through the blood-dust, away from the White River.

Eventually Corum spoke to Noreg-Dan. "Have you heard of this place before, King Noreg-Dan?"

He shook his head. "I never knew what really lay beyond the Blood Plain, but I did not expect this. Perhaps it is new…"

"New?" Rhalina looked curiously at him. "What do you mean?"

"Chaos is forever altering the landscape, playing new tricks with it—playing new jokes. Perhaps Queen Xiombarg knows that we are here. Perhaps she is playing a game with us…"

Jhary stroked his cat between its ears. "It would be like a Queen of Chaos to do such a thing, yet I suspect she would have planned worse than this for the destroyer of her brother."

"This could be just the beginning," Rhalina pointed out. "She could be building up to her true vengeance…"

"But I think not," Jhary insisted. "I have fought against Chaos in many worlds and in many guises and one thing that they are is impetuous. I think she would have acknowledged what she was doing by now if she knew who Prince Corum was. No, she still concentrates on the events taking place in the realm we have left. That is not to say we are not in danger," he added with a faint smile.

"In danger of starving again," Corum said. "If nothing else. This place is the most barren of all—and there is no way down, no way across, no way back…"

MICHAEL MOORCOCK

"We must keep moving until we do find a way down or a way across," Rhalina told him. "Surely the abyss must end somewhere?"

"Possibly," said Noreg-Dan, rubbing at his gaunt face, "but I remind you again that this is a realm completely ruled by Chaos. From what you have told me of Arioch's realm, he never wielded the power which Xiombarg wields—he was the least of the Sword Rulers. It is said that Mabelode, the King of the Swords, is even more powerful than she—that he has created of his realm a constantly shifting substance which changes shape more swiftly than thought…"

"Then I pray we are never forced to visit Mabelode," Jhary murmured. "This situation is sufficiently terrifying for me. I have witnessed Total Chaos and I like it not at all."

They tramped on beside the unchanging edge of the abyss.

Lost in a daze of weariness and monotony Corum only gradually began to realize that the sky was darkening. He looked up. Was the sun moving?

But the sun seemed to be in the same position. Instead, an eddy of black cloud had risen from somewhere and was streaming across the sky, heading towards the far side of the abyss. He had no means of knowing whether this were some sorcerous manifestation or if it were natural. He stopped. It had grown colder. Now the others noticed the clouds.

Noreg-Dan's eyes held trepidation. He drew his cracked leather coat about him and licked his bearded lips.

Suddenly, from Jhary's shoulder the little black-and-white cat leapt into the air and sped away on its black, white-tipped wings. It began to circle over the gorge, almost out of their range of vision. Jhary, too, looked perturbed, for the cat was behaving uncharacteristically.

Rhalina drew closer to Corum and put one hand on his

arm. He hugged her shoulders and stared skyward at the black streamers of cloud as they dashed from nowhere to nowhere.

"Have you seen such a sight before, King Noreg-Dan?" Corum called through the gloom. "Has it significance for you?"

Noreg-Dan shook his head. "No, I have not seen this before, but it has significance—it is an omen, I fear, of some danger from Chaos. I have seen similar sights."

"We had best be ready for what comes." Corum drew his long Vadhagh sword and threw back his scarlet robe to expose his silver byrnie. The others drew their own blades and stood there on the edge of that vast pit, waiting for whatever might come to threaten them.

Whiskers the cat was flying back. It was miaowing shrilly, urgently. It had seen something in the abyss. They stepped to the brink and peered over.

A reddish shadow moved in the yellow mist. Gradually it began to emerge; gradually its shape was defined.

It flew upon billowing crimson wings and its grinning face was that of a shark. It looked like something which should have inhabited the sea rather than the air and this was confirmed by the way in which it flew—with slow, undulating wings as if through liquid. Row upon row of sharp fangs filled its red mouth and its body was the size of a large bull, its wingspan nearly thirty feet.

Out of the frightful pit it came, its jaws opening and closing as if it already anticipated its feast. Its golden eyes burned with hunger and with rage.

"It is the Ghanh," said Noreg-Dan hopelessly. "The Ghanh which led the Chaos pack upon my country. It is one of Queen Xiombarg's favourite creations. It will take us before ever our swords strike a single blow."

"So you call it a Ghanh on this plane?" Jhary said with interest. "I have seen it before and, as I remember, I have seen it destroyed."

"How was it destroyed?" Corum asked him as the Ghanh flew higher and closer.

"That part I forget."

"If we spread out, we shall have a better chance," Corum said, backing away from the gorge's edge. "Quickly."

"If you'll forgive the suggestion, friend Corum," Jhary said as he, too, stepped backwards. "I think your netherworld allies would be of use to us here."

"Those allies are now the black birds we fought on the mountain. Could they defeat the Ghanh…?"

"I suggest you discover that now."

Corum flung up the eye-patch and peered again into the netherworld. There they were, a score of black, brooding birds, each with the mark of the barbed Vadhagh lance in its breast. But they saw Corum and they recognized him. One of them opened its beak and screeched in a tone so hopeless that Corum felt almost sympathetic to it.

"Can you understand me?" he said.

He heard Rhalina's voice. "It is almost upon us, Corum!"

"We—understand—master. Have you—a prize—for us?" said one of the birds.

Corum shuddered. "Aye, if you can take it."

The Hand of Kwll reached into that murky cavern and it beckoned to the birds. With a dreadful rustling sound they took to the air.

And they flew into the world in which Corum and his companions stood awaiting the Ghanh.

"There," said Corum. "There is your prize."

The black birds flung their wounded, dead-alive bodies

higher into the sky and began to wheel as the Ghanh swam over the edge of the gorge and opened its jaws, giving a piercing scream as it saw the four mortals.

"Run!" Corum shouted.

They took to their heels, scattering, running through the deep drifts of blood-dust as the Ghanh screamed again and hesitated, deciding which human to deal with first.

Corum choked on the stink of the creature as the wind of its breath touched him. He darted a look backward. He remembered how cowardly the birds had been, how they had taken long to make up their minds to attack him before. Would they have the courage—even though it meant their release from limbo—to attack the Ghanh?

But now the birds were spearing downwards again at an incredible speed. The Ghanh had not known they were there and it screamed in surprise as their beaks drove into its soft head. It snapped at them and seized two bodies in its jaws. Yet, though half-eaten by the creature, the beaks continued to peck, for the living dead could not be slain again.

The Ghanh's wings beat close to the ground and a huge cloud of blood-dust rose all around it. Through this dust Corum and the others could see the fray. The Ghanh leapt and twisted and snapped and screamed, but the black birds' beaks pecked relentlessly at its skull. The Ghanh reared and fell on its back. It twisted its wings so that it was rolled in them, trying to protect its head, and in this peculiar manner tumbled hither and thither across the dust. The black birds flapped into the air then descended again, trying to perch on the cocoon as it writhed about, still pecking. Streams of green blood poured from the Ghanh now and the blood-dust stuck to it so that it was all begrimed and tattered.

Then, quite suddenly, it had rolled over the edge of the abyss. The companions ran forward to see what had happened, the disturbed dust stinging their eyes and clogging their lungs. They saw the Ghanh falling. They saw its wings open and slow its descent, but it did not have the power to do more than drift back towards the floor of the pit as the black birds pecked and pecked at its exposed skull. The yellow mist swallowed them all.

Corum waited, but nothing emerged from the mist again.

"Does that mean that you have no more allies in the netherworld, Corum?" Jhary asked. "For the birds did not take their prey with them…"

Corum nodded. "I wonder the same." He lifted the eye-patch again and saw that the strange, cold cave was bare. "Aye—no allies there."

"So an impasse has been created. The birds have not killed the Ghanh and they have not themselves been destroyed," Jhary-a-Conel said. "Still, at least that danger has been averted. Let's press on."

The black clouds had ceased to stream across the sky but had instead stopped in their tracks and cut out the sunlight. Beneath this dark shroud they stumbled onward.

Corum noticed that Jhary had been brooding deeply since the birds had driven off the Ghanh and at last he said, "What is it that bothers you, Jhary-a-Conel?"

The man adjusted his wide hat on his head and pursed his lips. "It occurred to me that if the Ghanh was not slain but instead returned to its lair—and if the Ghanh is, as King Noreg-Dan says, a favourite pet of Queen Xiombarg's—then fairly soon now (if not already) Queen Xiombarg will become aware of our presence here. Doubtless if she becomes aware of us then she will decide to act to punish us for what we did to her pet…"

Corum removed his helmet and ran his gauntleted hand over his hair. He looked at the others who had stopped to listen to Jhary.

"It is true," said the King Without a Country with a sigh. "We must expect to have Queen Xiombarg upon us very soon—or, at the very least, some more of her minions if she is still not aware that her brother's destroyer is in her realm and thinks only that we are upstart mortals…"

Rhalina had been ahead of the rest. She hardly listened to the conversation but instead pointed just in front of her. "Look! Look!" she cried.

They ran towards her and saw that she pointed at a place on the edge of the abyss—a square-cut notch carved from the rock and larger than a man's body. They clustered around it and saw that a stairway led down and down into the distant mist. But the stairway was scarcely more than a foot across and it went straight beside the massive wall of the cliff until it disappeared into the mist a mile below. If one missed one's footing for an instant, then one would be plunged into the abyss.

Corum stood staring at the stairway. Had it just appeared? Was it a trick of Queen Xiombarg's? Would the steps suddenly vanish when they were halfway down—if they ever managed to get halfway down?

But the alternative was to continue to trudge along the edge and perhaps, ultimately, find themselves back at the White River (for Corum was beginning to suspect that the Blood Plain was circular, containing the Lake of Voices and the mountains, and that the abyss extended all around it).

With a sigh Corum gradually lowered himself to the first step and, on weakened legs, his back against the smooth rock, began to descend.

The four little figures inched their way down the slippery steps until the top of the abyss itself was lost in gloom, while the bottom was still shrouded by the yellow mist. There was a frightening silence as they moved. They dared not speak—dared not do anything which would break their concentration as they lowered themselves from step to step with the abyss seeming sometimes to draw them into its depths as their vertigo increased. All were shivering, for the rock chilled them, all were sure that after a few more steps they would lose their footing and plunge down into the yellow mist.

And then they began to hear it. It echoed from the mist. A grunting and a wheezing and a snorting and a cackling which increased as they descended.

Corum stopped and looked back at the others who lay against the rock and listened with him. Rhalina was closest to him, then Jhary and finally the King Without a Country.

It was Noreg-Dan who spoke first. "I know the sound," he said. "I have heard it before."

"What is it?" Rhalina whispered.

"It is the noise which Xiombarg's beasts make. I spoke of the Ghanh which led the Chaos pack. Well, those noises are the noises made by the Chaos pack. We should have guessed what lay beyond the yellow mist…"

Corum felt a great coldness grip him. He peered downwards to where the unseen Beasts of the Abyss awaited their coming.

4

THE CHARIOTS OF CHAOS

W HAT SHALL WE do?" Rhalina whispered. "What *can* we do against them?"

Corum said nothing. Carefully keeping his balance he drew his sword, steadying himself with his six-fingered, jeweled hand.

While the Ghanh lived and fought the black birds, there could be no help from the netherworld.

"Do you hear that now?" Jhary said. "That odd—creaking...?"

Corum nodded. With the creaking was a rumbling sound and it was vaguely familiar. It mingled with the snorts and the grunts and the bellows issuing from the yellow mist.

"There is nought for it," he said at length. "We must go on and hope that we reach the floor of the abyss soon. At least there we shall be less exposed and able to stand and fight whatever— whatever it is that makes the noise."

They continued their cautious descent, eyes wary for the first signs of the beasts.

* * *

Corum's foot had touched the floor of the abyss before he quite realized it. He had been climbing downwards for so long that he had become used to lying flat against the rock and feeling with his foot for each new step. Now there were no more steps and he could see the ground, uneven, covered in boulders, stretching away into the yellow mist, but he could see nothing that lived.

The others joined him as he peered forward. The grunts and the cackles continued and an appalling stink greeted their nostrils, but the source of the sounds and the stink was not yet visible. The creaking and the rumbling also continued.

Corum saw them at last.

"By Elric's Sword!" Jhary groaned. "Those are the Chariots of Chaos. I should have guessed!"

Monstrous lumbering chariots drawn by reptilian beasts were beginning to emerge from the mist. They were filled by a variety of creatures, some even mounted on others' backs. Each beast was a travesty of a human being—each was clad in armour and bore a weapon of some kind. Here were piglike, doglike, cowlike, froglike, horselike things, some more deformed than others— animals warped into parodies of humanity.

"Did Chaos turn these beasts into what they are now?" Corum gasped.

Jhary said, "You are mistaken, Corum."

"What mean you?"

The King Without a Country spoke up. "These beasts," he said, "were once men. Many of them were my subjects who sided with Chaos because they saw that it was more powerful than Law…"

"And that transformation was their reward?" Rhalina said in disgust.

"They are probably not aware of the transformation," Jhary told her quietly. "They have degenerated too much. They retain little memory of their former existences."

The black chariots creaked closer, bearing their grunting, shrieking, bellowing crews.

There was nothing for it but to turn and run from the chariots, dashing over the uneven ground, swords in hand, coughing on the stink of the Chaos pack and the clinging, yellow mist.

The Chaos pack howled in delight and whipped up their reptilian beasts and the chariots began to move faster. The ghastly, deformed army was enjoying the hunt.

Weakened by their earlier adventures and their lack of food or drink, the four companions could not run swiftly and at last, behind a large boulder, they were forced to rest. The chariots rumbled on towards them, bringing the cacophony, the hellish once-human things, the nauseating smells.

Corum hoped that the chariots would pass them by but the Chaos pack could see more easily through the mist and the first chariot turned towards them. Corum began to climb the boulder to get above the chariot. He struck out with his fist as a pig-thing clambered after him. The fist sank into the creature's face and was held there while the thing drew its own brass-studded club and raised its arm to finish Corum. Corum stabbed with his sword and the pig-thing shuddered, fell back. Now the others were under attack. Rhalina defended herself well with her own sword. They stood around the base of the boulder on the opposite side to Corum while he defended their rear. A dog-thing leapt at him. It wore a helmet and a breastplate but its muzzle was full of long teeth which snapped at his arm. He swung the sword and broke that muzzle in a single, smashing blow. Hands which had turned into claws and paws grabbed at him, tore at his cloak, his boots. Swords stabbed and clubs struck the stone at his feet as a whole mass of the creatures began to climb towards him. He stamped on fingers, hacked off limbs, drove his sword through mouths and eyes and hearts and all the time was filled with a sickening panic which only made him fight harder.

The babble of the Chaos pack seemed to grow louder and louder in his ears. Their chariots kept appearing out of the mist until several hundred of the things surrounded the boulder.

Then it came clear to Corum that the pack did not intend, at this stage, to kill them. If they had wished to they could have slain him and his companions by now. Doubtless they planned to torture them in some way—or perhaps turn them into the same kind of creatures that they had become.

Corum remembered the Mabden tortures with horror and he fought all the harder, hoping to drive some member of the Chaos pack to kill him.

But slowly the fearsome tide rolled in until so many corpses pressed about the base of the boulder that Corum's three friends were unable to move their arms and were trapped. Only Corum fought on, hacking at all who sought to take him, and then something clambered over the rocks behind him and seized his legs, dragging him down to where Rhalina, Jhary and the King Without a Country stood, disarmed and bound.

A creature with the lopsided face of a horse swaggered through the ranks of the Chaos pack and curled its lips to reveal huge brown teeth. It gave a whinnying laugh and set its helmet jauntily on its head, its hairy thumbs hooked in the belt around its belly.

"Should we save you for ourselves," it said, "or take you to our mistress? Queen Xiombarg might be interested in you…"

"Why should she be interested in four mortal travelers?" Corum asked.

The horse-thing grinned at him. "Perhaps you are more than that? Perhaps you are agents of Law?"

"You know that Law no longer rules here!"

"But Law may *wish* to rule again—you may have been sent here from another realm."

"Do you not recognize me!" cried King Noreg-Dan.

The horse-thing scratched at its forelock and peered stupidly at the King Without a Country. "Why should I recognize you?"

"Because I recognize you. I see the traces of your original features…"

"Be silent! I do not know what you mean!" The horse-thing half drew its dagger from its belt. "Be silent!"

"Because you cannot bear to remember!" shouted the King Without a Country. "You were Polib-Bav, Count of Tern! You threw in your lot with Chaos even before my country fell…"

A look of fear came into the horse-thing's eyes. It shook its head and snorted. "No!"

"You are Polib-Bav and you were betrothed to my daughter— the girl whom your Chaos pack—aaagh! I cannot bear to remember that horror!"

"You remember nothing," said Polib-Bav thickly. "I say I am just what I am."

"What is your name?" Noreg-Dan said. "What is your name, if it is not Polib-Bav, Count of Tern?"

The horse-thing struck out at the king's face with its clumsy hand. "What if I am? My loyalty is to Queen Xiombarg, not to you."

"I would not have you serve me," sneered the king as blood

welled on his upper lip. "Oh, look what has become of you, Polib-Bav."

The horse-thing turned away. "I live," it said. "I command this legion."

"A legion of pathetic monsters!" Jhary laughed.

A cow-thing kicked at Jhary's groin with its hoof and the companion to champions groaned. But he lifted his head and laughed again. "This degeneration is only the beginning. I have seen what mortals who serve Chaos become—foulness, nothingness—shapeless horrors!"

Polib-Bav scratched its head and said more softly, "What of that? The decision was made. It cannot be revoked. Queen Xiombarg promises us eternal life."

"It will be eternal," Jhary said. "But it will not be life. I have travelled to many planes during many ages and I have seen what Chaos comes to—barrenness. That alone is eternal, unless Law can save it."

"Faugh!" said the horse-thing. "Put them in the chariot—in my chariot—and we shall carry them to Queen Xiombarg."

King Noreg-Dan tried to appeal again to Polib-Bav. "You were once handsome, Count of Tern. My daughter loved you and you loved her. You were loyal to me in those days."

Polib-Bav turned away. "And now I am loyal to Queen Xiombarg. This is her realm now. Lord Shalod of Law has fled and shall never rule here again. His armies and his allies were destroyed, as you well know, on the Plain of Blood..." Polib-Bav pointed upwards. He accepted the four swords which a frog-thing handed him and tucked them under his arm. "Into the chariot with them. We ride for Queen Xiombarg's palace."

As he was forced to enter Polib-Bav's chariot with the others Corum was in despair. His hands were tied behind his back with strong cords, he could see no way of escape. Once he was taken before Queen Xiombarg she would recognize him. She would destroy him as she would destroy the rest and all hope of saving Lywm-an-Esh would be gone. With King Lyr victorious, the forces of Chaos would begin to gather strength. Another Sword Ruler would be summoned and the Fifteen Planes would be wholly in the control of the Lords of Entropy.

He lay at Polib-Bav's feet now, side by side with his friends, as the Chariots of Chaos began to move along the floor of the abyss, wheels creaking and groaning, bumping over the loose rocks. And soon Corum had lost consciousness.

He awoke blinking in stronger light. The mist was gone. He lifted his head and saw that a great cliff towered behind them. He guessed that they had left the abyss. They seemed to be moving through a sparse forest of sickly, leprous trees which had caught some blight. He moved his bruised head and stared into the face of Rhalina. She had been weeping but now she attempted to smile at him.

"We left the abyss through a tunnel some hours back," she told him. "It must be a long way to Queen Xiombarg's palace. I wonder why they do not use swifter, more sorcerous means to go there?"

"Chaos is whimsical," said a voice behind her. It was Jhary-a-Conel's. "And in a timeless world there is no need for swiftness in such matters."

"What has become of your little cat?" Corum murmured.

"It was wiser than I: it flew off. I did not see—"

"Silence!" bellowed the voice of the horse-thing driving the chariot. "Your babbling annoys me."

"Perhaps it disturbs you," Jhary ventured. "Perhaps it reminds you that you could once think coherently, speak well…"

Polib-Bav kicked him in the face and he spluttered as the blood gushed from his nose.

Corum growled and vainly tried to free himself. Polib-Bav's horse face looked down at him and laughed. "You're grotesque enough, yourself, friend—with that eye and that hand grafted onto you. If I had not known better, I'd have said you served Chaos."

"Perhaps I do," Corum said. "You did not ask. You merely assumed that I served Law."

Polib-Bav frowned, but then his stupid face cleared. "You are trying to trick me. I will do nothing until Queen Xiombarg has seen you…" He shook the reins and the reptilian beasts began to move faster, "… after all, it is almost certain that it was you and your friends who killed the strongest member of our legion. We saw it attacked and we saw it vanish."

"You speak of the Ghanh?" Corum asked, his spirits beginning to lift. "Of the Ghanh!"

And, at that moment, the Hand of Kwll moved once more of its own volition and snapped the cords binding Corum's wrists.

"You see!" said Polib-Bav in triumph. "It was I who tricked you. You knew the Ghanh was slain. Therefore it could only have been… What! You are free!" He hauled on the reins. "Stop!" He drew his sword, but Corum had rolled over the floor of the chariot and leapt to the ground. He pushed back his eye-patch and at once saw the netherworld cave from which his allies had issued in the past. There, with its head a ruin of congealed blood, lay the Ghanh.

The Hand of Kwll moved into the netherworld as Polib-Bav's creatures advanced on Corum. It beckoned to the Ghanh which moved its dead head very reluctantly.

"You must do my bidding," Corum said. "And then you will be free. You must take many prizes to pay for your release."

The Ghanh did not speak, but it gave a scream from its fanged jaws as if to acknowledge that it had heard.

"Come!" Corum cried. "Come—take your prizes."

And the Ghanh's crimson wings began to beat as it flapped slowly from the cave, leaving the netherworld behind it and coming back, once again, into the world from which the birds had but lately banished it.

"The Ghanh has come back!" Polib-Bav shouted in triumph. "Oh, lovely Ghanh, thou hast returned to us!"

The Chaos pack had seized Corum again, but now he was smiling as, with a tortured screech, the Ghanh's great body engulfed a nearby chariot and its strange wings wrapped themselves around the whole thing and began to crush the occupants to death.

So astonished were the Chaos beasts holding Corum that he was able to tug himself free. They came after him but he turned and the Hand of Kwll smashed into the face of one, cracked another's collarbone. He raced for Polib-Bav's chariot. The leader of the beasts had left his chariot and stood beside it, his huge, horse's eyes fixed on what was happening to his companions. Before he had really noticed Corum, the Prince in the Scarlet Robe had grabbed his sword from the pile on the floor of the chariot and aimed a blow at Polib-Bav. The horse-thing jumped back, drawing his own sword. But his movements were dazed and clumsy. He parried, tried to stab, missed as Corum dodged aside, and received the Vadhagh metal in his throat. Choking, he died.

Quickly Corum cut the bonds of his friends and they, too, retrieved their swords, ready to fight the Chaos creatures. But the pack, recovering from its initial horror, was fleeing. Its chariots raced hither and yon through the pale, sickly trees as the Ghanh left its first victims and pursued some more. Corum bent and stripped the corpse of Polib-Bav, taking his water bottle and the pouch of coarse bread at his belt. Soon the Chaos pack had disappeared and they were left alone on the road through the forest.

Corum inspected the chariot. The reptiles seemed passive enough.

"Could we drive this, do you think, King Noreg-Dan?" he asked.

The King Without a Country shook his head dubiously. "I am not sure. Perhaps..."

"I think I could drive it," Jhary told them. "I've had a little experience of such chariots and the creatures which pull them." His sack bouncing at his belt, the wide brim of his hat waving, he jumped into the chariot, taking up the reins. He turned and grinned at them. "Where would you go? Still to Xiombarg's palace?"

Corum laughed. "Not yet, I think. She'll send for us when she learns what became of her pack. We'll take that direction, I think." He pointed away through the trees. He helped Rhalina into the chariot, then waited while King Noreg-Dan climbed aboard. Finally, he got in himself. Jhary shook the reins, turned the chariot and soon it had bounced through the leprous forest and was rolling down a hill towards a valley full of what seemed to be upright, slender stones.

5

THE FROZEN ARMY

THEY WERE NOT stones.

They were men.

Each man a warrior—each warrior frozen like a statue, his weapons in his hands.

"This," said Noreg-Dan in quiet awe, "is the Frozen Army. The last army to take arms against Chaos…"

"Was this its punishment?" Corum asked.

"Aye."

Jhary, gripping the reins, said, "They live? Is that so? They know that we pass through their ranks?"

"Aye. I heard that Queen Xiombarg said that since they supported Law so wholeheartedly they should have a taste of what Law aimed for—they should know the ultimate in tranquility," Noreg-Dan said.

Rhalina shivered. "Is this really what Law comes to?"

"So Chaos would have us believe," Jhary said. "But it matters not, for the Cosmic Balance requires equilibrium—something of Chaos, something of Law—so that each stabilizes the other. The difference is that Law acknowledges the authority of the Balance, while Chaos would deny it. But Chaos cannot deny that authority completely for its adherents know that to disobey some things is to be destroyed. Thus Queen Xiombarg dare not enter the realm of another Great Old God and, as in the case of your realm, must work through others. She, like the rest, must also watch her dealings with mortals, for they cannot be destroyed by her willy-nilly—there are rules…"

"But no rules to protect these poor creatures," Rhalina said.

"Some. They have not died. She has not killed them."

Corum remembered the tower where he had found Arioch's heart. There, too, had been frozen men.

"Unless directly attacked," Jhary explained, "Xiombarg cannot kill mortals. But she can use those loyal to her to kill other mortals, do you see, and she can suspend the lives of warriors like these."

"So we are safe from Queen Xiombarg," Corum said.

"If you choose to think so." Jhary smiled. "You are by no means safe from her minions and, as you have seen, she has many of those."

"Aye," said the King Without a Country feelingly. "Aye. Many."

Holding his reins in one hand Jhary dusted at his clothes. They were tattered and bloodstained from the various flesh wounds he had sustained in the battle with the Chaos pack. "I would give much for a new suit," he murmured. "I'd make a bargain with Xiombarg herself…"

"We mention that name too often," King Noreg-Dan said nervously as he clung to the side of the jolting chariot. "We shall bring her down on us if we are not more discreet."

Then the sky laughed.

Golden light began to dapple the clouds. A brilliant orange

aura sprang up in the distance ahead and cast giant shadows for the frozen warriors.

Jhary jerked the chariot to a halt, his face suddenly pale.

Purple brilliance came from the sky in fragments the size of raindrops.

And the laughter went on and on.

"What is it?" Rhalina's hand went to her sword.

The King Without a Country put his haggard face in his hands and his shoulders slumped. "It is she. I warned you. It is she."

"Xiombarg?" Corum drew his own sword. "Is it Xiombarg, Noreg-Dan?"

"Aye, it is she."

The ground shook with the laughter. Several of the frozen warriors toppled and fell, still in the same positions. Corum looked about for the source of the laughter. Was it in the aura? Or in the golden light? Or the purple rain?

"Where are you, Queen Xiombarg!" He brandished his sword. His mortal eye flashed his defiance. "Where are you, Creature of Evil?"

"I AM EVERYWHERE!" answered a huge, sweet voice. "I AM THIS REALM AND THIS REALM IS XIOMBARG OF CHAOS!"

"We are surely doomed," stuttered the King Without a Country.

"You said she could not attack us," Corum said to Jhary-a-Conel.

"I said she could not directly attack us. But see…"

Corum looked. Over the valley now came hopping things. They hopped on several legs and from their bodies sprouted a dozen or more tentacles. Their huge eyes rolled, their massive fangs clashed.

"The Karmanal of Zert," Jhary said in mild surprise as he

dropped the reins and armed himself with sword and poignard. "I have encountered these before."

"How did you escape them?" Rhalina asked.

"I was at that time companion to a champion who had the power to destroy them."

"I, too, have a power," Corum said grimly, raising his hand to his eye. But Jhary shook his head and grimaced.

"I fear not. The Karmanal of Zert are indestructible. Both Law and Chaos have, in their time, taken steps to do away with them—they are fickle creatures who fight for one side or another without apparent reason. They have no souls, no true existence."

"Therefore they should not be able to harm us!"

The laughter rang on.

"I agree that, logically, they should not be able to harm us," Jhary answered equably. "But I am afraid that they can."

About ten of the hopping creatures were nearing their chariot, weaving between the statuelike warriors.

And they were singing.

"The Karmanal of Zert always sing before they feast," Jhary told them. "Always."

Corum wondered if Jhary had gone mad. The tentacled monsters were almost upon them and the companion to champions continued to chat without apparent awareness of their danger.

The singing was harmonious and somehow made the creatures even more terrifying while, as a counterpoint, Xiombarg's laughter continued to fill the sky.

When the hopping things were almost upon them Jhary raised his hands, dagger in one, sword in the other, and cried, "Queen Xiombarg! Queen Xiombarg! Who do you think you would destroy?"

The Karmanal of Zert stopped suddenly, as frozen as the army which surrounded them.

"I destroy a few mortals who have set themselves against me, who have caused the deaths of those I loved," said a voice from behind them.

Corum turned to see the most beautiful woman who had ever existed. Her hair was dark gold with streaks of red and black, her face was perfection and her eyes and lips offered a thousand times more than any woman had offered a man in the whole of history. Her body was tall and of exquisite shape, clothed in drapes of gold and orange and purple. She smiled tenderly at him.

"Is that what I destroy?" she murmured. "Then what do I destroy, Master Timeras?"

"I am called Jhary-a-Conel now," he said pleasantly. "May I introduce...?"

Corum stepped forward. "Have you betrayed us, Jhary? Are you in league with Chaos?"

"He is not, sadly, in league with Chaos," said Queen Xiombarg. "But I know he rides often with those who serve Law." She looked at him affectionately. "You do not change, Timeras, basically. And I like you best as a man, I think."

"And I like you best as a woman, Xiombarg."

"As a woman I must rule this realm. I know you for a sometime hero's lickspittle, Jhary-Timeras, and assume this handsome Vadhagh with his strange eye and hand is a hero of sorts..."

She glared suddenly at Corum.

"Now I know!"

Corum drew himself up.

"NOW I KNOW!"

Her shape began to alter. It began to flow outwards and upwards. Her face was that of a skull, then that of a bird, then that of a man, until at last it reverted to that of a beautiful woman. But now Xiombarg stood a hundred feet high and her expression was no longer tender.

"NOW I KNOW!"

Jhary laughed. "May I, as I said, introduce Prince Corum Jhaelen Irsei—he of the Scarlet Robe?"

"HOW DO YOU DARE ENTER MY REALM—YOU WHO DESTROYED MY BROTHER? EVEN NOW THOSE STILL LOYAL TO ME IN MY BROTHER'S REALM ARE SEEKING FOR YOU. YOU ARE FOOLISH, MORTAL. AH, THE IGNOMINY. I THOUGHT A BRAVE HERO BANISHED MY BROTHER—BUT NOW I KNOW IT WAS A MORON! KARMANAL CREATURES—BEGONE!" The hopping things vanished. "I WILL HAVE A SWEETER VENGEANCE ON YOU, CORUM JHAELEN IRSEI—AND ON ALL WHO TRAVEL WITH YOU!"

The golden light faded, the orange aura disappeared and the purple rain ceased to fall, but Xiombarg's huge shape still flickered there in the sky. "I SWEAR THIS BY THE COSMIC BALANCE—I WILL RETURN WHEN I HAVE CONSIDERED THE FORM OF MY VENGEANCE. I WILL FOLLOW YOU WHEREVER YOU TRY TO ESCAPE. AND I WILL GIVE YOU CAUSE TO WISH THAT YOU HAD NEVER ENCOUNTERED LORD ARIOCH OF CHAOS AND THUS WON THE ANGER OF HIS SISTER XIOMBARG!"

Xiombarg faded and silence returned.

Corum, much shaken, turned to Jhary. "Why did you tell her? Now there is no escape for us! She has promised to pursue us wherever we go—you heard her. Why did you do it?"

"I thought she was about to find out," Jhary said mildly. "Also it was the only way to save us."

"To save us!"

"Aye. Now the Karmanal of Zert no longer threaten us. I assure you that we should have been in their bellies by now if I had not spoken to Queen Xiombarg. I guessed that she could not know very well what you looked like—most of us seem very alike to the gods—but that she might learn when we fought. Corum—it was the only way to stop the Karmanal."

"But it has done us no good. Now she goes to summon whatever horrors she plans to set upon us. Soon she will return and we shall suffer a worse fate."

"I must admit," said Jhary, "that there was another consideration. Now we have time to see what this is coming yonder."

They looked.

It was something that flew and flashed and droned.

"What is it?" Corum asked.

"It is, I believe, a ship of the air," said Jhary. "I hope it has come to save us."

"Perhaps it has come to harm us?" Corum said reasonably enough. "I still feel you should not have revealed who I was, Jhary…"

"It is always best to bring these things out into the open," Jhary said cheerfully.

6

THE CITY IN THE PYRAMID

THE SHIP OF the air had a hull of blue metal in which were set enamels and ceramics of various rich colours, making a number of complicated designs. It brought a slight smell of almonds with it as it began to descend, and its moan was almost like that of a human voice.

Now Corum could see its brass rails, its steel, silver and platinum fixtures, its ornate wheelhouse, and he felt that he was reminded of something by it—an image, perhaps, of childhood. He stared curiously at it as it began to land and a small object rose up from it and flew towards them.

It was Jhary's cat.

Suddenly Corum stared at Jhary and laughed. The cat came and settled on the shoulder of the companion to heroes and it nuzzled his ear.

"You sent the cat to find help when the Chaos pack set upon us!" Rhalina said before Corum could speak. "That is why you told Xiombarg who Corum was—for you knew that help was coming and thought your plan thwarted at the last moment."

Jhary shrugged. "I did not know the cat would find help, but I guessed."

"From where has that strange flying craft come?" asked the King Without a Country.

"Why, where else but from the City in the Pyramid? It was my instruction to the cat to look for it. I would gather that it found it."

"And how did it communicate with the folk of that city?" Corum asked as they drew nearer to the blue ship of the air.

"In emergencies, as you know, the cat can communicate quite clearly with me. In a very serious emergency it will use more energy and communicate with whom it pleases."

Whiskers purred and licked Jhary's face with its little rough tongue. He murmured something to it and smiled. Then he said to Corum, "We'd best hurry, though, for Xiombarg may begin to wonder why I did reveal your name. It is one of the characteristics of many of the Chaos Lords that they are impetuous and not given overmuch to thinking."

The ship of the air was a good forty feet long and had seats running the whole of its length on both sides. It appeared to be empty, but then a tall, comely man stepped from the wheelhouse and came forward towards them. He was smiling at Corum's complete astonishment.

For the steersman of the ship of the air was quite plainly of no other race but Corum's. He was a Vadhagh. His skull was long, his slanting eyes purple and gold, his ears pointed and his body slender and delicate but containing a great deal of energy.

"Welcome, Corum in the Scarlet Robe," he said. "I have come to take you to Gwlās-cor-Gwrys, the one bastion this realm has against that Chaos creature you have just met."

Dazed, Corum Jhaelen Irsei entered the ship of the air while the steersman continued to smile at his astonishment.

They took their places near the wheelhouse in the stern and the tall Vadhagh made the ship rise slowly and begin to head in the direction it had come. Rhalina looked backward at the forest of frozen warriors they left behind. "Is there nothing we could do to help those poor souls?" she asked Jhary.

"Only help make Law strong in our own realm so that it can one day send aid to this realm, just as Chaos now sends aid to ours," Jhary told her.

They were soon crossing a land of oozing stuff which flung up tendrils at them and sought to drag them down into itself. Sometimes faces appeared in the stuff, sometimes hands raised as if in supplication. "A Chaos sea," King Noreg-Dan told them. "There are several such places in the realm now. Some say that that is what those mortals who serve Chaos finally degenerate to."

"I have seen its like," nodded Jhary.

Strange forests passed below them and valleys filled with perpetually burning fire. They saw rivers of molten metal and beautiful castles made all of jewels. Horrid flying creatures sometimes rushed into the air towards them but turned aside when they recognized the craft, though it was apparently without protection.

"These people must have a powerful sorcery to make boats fly," Rhalina whispered to Corum. And Corum made no reply at first, for he was deep in thought, racking his memory.

At last he spoke. "This is not sorcery, as such," he told her. "It requires no spells and few incantations but is instead mechanical in its nature. Certain forces are harnessed to give power to machines—some of them much more delicate than anything the Mabden could imagine—which propel such vessels through the air and do many other things. Some of the machines could once sunder the fabric of the Wall Between the Realms and pass easily from plane to plane. My ancestors are said to have created such machines but most chose not to use them, preferring a different logic to their living. I dimly remember a legend which says that one Sky City—that was the name they gave to their cities—left our realm altogether, to explore the other worlds of the multiverse. Perhaps there was more than one such city, for I know that one did destroy itself when it went out of control during the Battle of Broggfythus and crashed close to Castle Erorn, as I told you. Perhaps another city was called Gwlās-cor-Gwrys and is now known as the City in the Pyramid."

Prince Corum was smiling joyfully and speaking excitedly. With his mortal hand he pressed Rhalina's arm. "Oh, Rhalina, can you understand what I feel at finding that some of my race still live, that Glandyth did not destroy them all?"

She smiled back at him. "I think so, Corum."

The air about them began to vibrate and the boat shuddered. The steersman called from the wheelhouse, "Do not be afraid. We are passing into another plane."

"Does that mean we are escaping Xiombarg?" asked the King Without a Country eagerly.

Jhary answered him. "No. Xiombarg's realm extends for five planes and we are merely going from one of those into a different one. Or so I would think."

The quality of the light changed and they looked over the side of the ship. A multicoloured gas swirled below them.

"The raw stuff of Chaos," said Jhary. "Queen Xiombarg has, as yet, made nothing with it."

They crossed the great gas and flew over a range of mountains, each more than a thousand feet high, but each one a perfect cube. Beyond the mountains was a dark jungle and beyond that a crystalline desert. The crystals of the desert moved constantly, their motion creating a tinkling music which was not pleasant. Among these crystals moved ochre beasts of enormous proportions but of primitive development. They were feeding off the crystals.

Then the crystal desert gave way to a flat, black plain and they saw ahead of them the City in the Pyramid.

The city was, in fact, a many-sided ziggurat. On each terrace were a large number of houses. Flowers, shrubs and trees grew along the terraces and the streets teemed with people. Over the whole city a greenish light flickered and the light took the form of a pyramid, enclosing the ziggurat. As the ship of the air flew towards it, a darker oval of green appeared in the flickering light and through this the ship passed. It circled the topmost building—a many-towered castle built all of metal—and then began to descend until it landed on a raised platform on the castle's battlements. Corum shouted with pleasure as he saw the gathering which welcomed him.

"They are my people!" he exclaimed to his companions. "They are all my people!"

The steersman left the wheelhouse and put his hand on Corum's shoulder. He signed to the men and women below and suddenly they were no longer on the ship of the air but were standing with the group, beneath the platform, looking up at the faces of Rhalina, Jhary and the King Without a Country as they peered over the rail of the ship in astonishment.

Corum was equally astonished to see the three suddenly vanish and appear beside him. One of the group then stepped forward. He was a thin, ancient man with a straight bearing, dressed in a thick robe and holding a staff.

"Welcome," he said, "to Law's last bastion."

* * *

Later they sat around a table of beautifully fashioned ruby-metal and listened to the old man who had introduced himself as Prince Yurette Hasdun Nury, Commander of Gwlās-cor-Gwrys, the City in the Pyramid. He had explained how Corum's speculations were substantially correct.

As they had eaten he had explained how Corum's people had chosen to remain in their castles after the Battle of Broggfythus and devote themselves to learning while his people had decided to take their Sky City and try to fly it beyond the Five Planes, through the Wall Between the Realms. They had succeeded, but had failed to return due to some power loss which they could not then restore. Since then they had managed only to explore these five planes and then, when the struggle between Law and Chaos had begun to build, they had remained neutral.

"We were fools to do so. We thought we were above such disputes. And slowly we saw Law conquered and Chaos emerge in all its grisly triumph to create its travesties of beauty. But by that time, though we did take our city against Xiombarg's creatures, we were too late. Chaos had gained all power and we could not fight it. Xiombarg sent—and still sends—armies against us. These we resisted, not without danger. And now it is stalemate. Every so often Xiombarg will send another army—some frightful, monstrous army—and we are forced to fight it. But we can do no more than that. I fear we are all that is left of Law, save you."

"Law has regained its power in our Five Planes," Corum told him. He described his adventures, his battle with Arioch and the final result which was to restore Lord Arkyn to his realm. "But that, too, is threatened for Law has still only a slender hold on the realm and all the forces of Chaos are being brought to bear on it."

"But Law still has some power!" Prince Yurette said. "We did not know that. We learned that the Sword Rulers controlled all the realms. If only we could return—take our city back through the Wall Between the Realms—and give you our aid. But we cannot. We have tried so often. The materials are not available on these planes for building up the massive power it needs."

"And if you had these materials?" Corum asked. "How long would it be before you could return to our realm?"

"Not long. But we are weakening already. A few more of Xiombarg's attacks—perhaps just one massive one—and we shall be destroyed."

Corum stared bitterly at the table. Was he to find Vadhagh folk still living only to see them die—crushed, as his family was crushed by the forces of Chaos?

"We had hoped to take you back with us, to relieve Lywm-an-Esh," he said. "But now we learn that is impossible and, it seems, we, too, are stranded in this realm, unable to go to the aid of our friends."

"If we had those rare minerals…" Prince Yurette paused. "But you could get them for us."

"We cannot return," Jhary-a-Conel pointed out. "We cannot get back to our realm. If it were possible, of course we could find the materials you need—or at least try to do so—but even then we could not be sure of being able to return here…"

Prince Yurette frowned. "It would be possible for us to send just one sky ship through the Wall Between the Realms. We have the power to do that, though it would dangerously weaken our defenses here. Yet it is worth the risk, I think."

Corum's spirits lifted. "Aye, Prince Yurette—anything is worth the risk if the cause of Law is to be saved."

* * *

While Prince Yurette conferred with his scientists, the four companions wandered through the marvelous city of Gwlās-cor-Gwrys. It was all made of metal—but metals so magnificent, so strange in texture and so rich in colour that even Corum could not guess at how they had been manufactured. Towers, domes, trellises, arches and pathways were of these metals, as were the ramps and stairways between the terraces. Everything in the city functioned independently of the outside world. Even the air was created within the confines of the shimmering pyramid of green light which cast its glow on all the outer flanks of Gwlās-cor-Gwrys.

And everywhere did the folk of the City in the Pyramid go about their day-to-day business. Some tended gardens and others saw to the distribution of food. There were many artists at work, performing musical compositions or displaying the pictures they had made—pictures on silk and marble and glass very similar in technique to those produced by Corum's own Vadhagh folk, but often with different styles and subjects, some of which Corum could not find it in him to like, perhaps because they were so strange.

They were shown the huge, beautiful machines which kept the city alive. They were shown its armaments, which protected it from the attacks of Chaos, the bays where its ships of the air were kept. They saw its schools and its restaurants and its theatres, its museums and its art galleries. And here was everything which Corum thought destroyed for ever by Glandyth-a-Krae and his barbarians. But now all this, too, was threatened with destruction—and destruction from the same source, ultimately.

They slept, they ate and their tattered, battered clothes were copied by the tailors and arms-smiths of Gwlās-cor-Gwrys so that when they awoke they found themselves with fresh raiment identical to that which they had worn upon starting out on their quest for the city.

Jhary-a-Conel was particularly pleased by this example of the city's hospitality and when, at last, they were invited to attend upon Prince Yurette, he expressed that gratitude roundly.

"The sky ship is ready," said Prince Yurette gravely. "You must go quickly now, for Queen Xiombarg, I learn, mounts a great attack upon us."

"Will you be able to withstand it with your power weakened?" Jhary asked.

"I hope so."

The King Without a Country stepped forward. "Forgive me, Prince Yurette, but I would stay here with you. If Law is to battle Chaos in my own realm, then I would battle with it."

Yurette inclined his head. "It shall be as you wish. But now hurry, Prince Corum. The sky ship awaits you on the roof. Stand on that mosaic circle there and you will be transported to the ship. Farewell!"

They stood within the mosaic circle on the prince's floor and, a heartbeat later, were once again upon the deck of the ornate flying craft.

The steersman was the same who had first greeted them.

"I am Bwydyth-a-Horn," he said. "Please sit where you sat before and cling tightly to the rail."

"Look!" Corum pointed beyond the green pyramid, out across the black plain. The huge shape of Queen Xiombarg could be seen again, her face alive with fury. And beneath her there marched a vast army, a foul army of fiends.

Then the sky ship had entered the air and sailed through

the dark green oval into a world which rang with the voices of the fiends.

And over all these voices sounded the hideous, vengeful laughter of Queen Xiombarg of Chaos.

"BEFORE I MERELY TOYED WITH THEM BECAUSE I ENJOYED THE GAME! BUT NOW THAT THEY HARBOUR THE DESTROYER OF MY BROTHER, THEY WILL PERISH IN BLACK AGONY!"

The air began to vibrate, a green globe of light now encircled the ship. The City in the Pyramid, the army of hell, Queen Xiombarg, all faded. The ship rocked crazily up and down, the moaning increased in pitch until it became a painful whine.

And then they had left the Realm of Queen Xiombarg and came again to the Realm of Arkyn of Law.

They sailed over the land of Lywm-an-Esh and it was not very different from the world they had just left. Chaos, here too, was on the march.

BOOK THREE

IN WHICH PRINCE CORUM AND HIS
COMPANIONS WAGE WAR, WIN A
VICTORY AND WONDER AT THE
WAYS OF LAW

THE HORDE FROM HELL

THICK SMOKE COILED from blazing villages, towns and cities. They were to the south-east of the River Ogyn in the Duchy of Kernow-a-Laun and it was plain that one of King Lyr-a-Brode's armies had landed on the coast, well south of Moidel's Mount.

"I wonder if Glandyth has yet discovered our leaving," Corum said as he stared miserably from the sky ship at the burning land. Crops had been destroyed, corpses lay rotting in the summer sun, even animals had been needlessly slaughtered. Rhalina was sickened by what had happened to her country and she could not look at it for long.

"Doubtless he has," she said quietly. "Their army has plainly been on the march for some time."

From time to time they saw small parties of barbarians in chariots or riding shaggy ponies, looting what was left of the settlements, though there was none left for them to slay or torture. Sometimes, too, they saw the refugees streaming southwards towards the mountains where doubtless they hoped to find a hiding place.

When, finally, they came to the River Ogyn itself it was clogged with death. Corpses of whole families rotted in the river, along with cattle, dogs and horses. The barbarians were ranging widely, following the main army, making sure that nothing lived where it had passed. And now Rhalina was weeping openly and Corum and Jhary were grim-faced as they strove to keep the stink of death from their nostrils and fretted that the sky ship, moving faster than any horse could, did not move more swiftly.

And then they saw the farmhouse.

Children were running inside the house, shepherded by their father who was armed with an old, rusty broadsword. The mother was putting up crude barricades.

Corum saw the source of their fear. A party of barbarians, about a dozen strong, was riding down the valley towards the farm. They had brands in their hands and were riding rapidly, whooping and roaring.

Corum had seen Mabden like these. He had been captured by them, tortured by them. They were no different from Glandyth-a-Krae's Denledhyssi, save that they rode ponies instead of chariots. They wore filthy furs and bore captured bracelets and necklaces all over them, their braids laced with ribbons of jewels.

He got up and went into the wheelhouse. "We must go down," he said harshly to Bwydyth-a-Horn. "There is a family—it is about to be attacked..."

Bwydyth looked at him sadly. "But there is so little time, Prince Corum." He tapped his jerkin. "We have to get this list of substances to Halwyg-nan-Vake if we are to rescue the city and, in turn, save Lywm-an-Esh..."

"Go down," Corum ordered.

Bwydyth said softly, "Very well." And he made adjustments to the controls, looking through a viewer which showed him the country below. "That farm?"

"Aye—that farm."

The sky ship began to descend. Corum went out on deck to watch. The barbarians had seen the ship and were pointing upwards in consternation, reining in their ponies. The ship began to circle towards the farmyard where there was barely space for it to land. Chickens ran squawking as its shadow fell on them. A pig scampered into its sty.

The ship's moaning dropped in pitch as it descended.

"Have your sword ready, Master Jhary," Corum said.

Jhary's sword was already in his hand. "There are ten or more of them," he cautioned. "Two of us. Will you use your powers?"

"I hope not. I am disgusted by all that is of Chaos."

"But, two against ten…"

"There is the steersman. And the farmer."

Jhary pursed his lips but said no more. The ship bumped to the ground. The steersman emerged holding a long pole-axe.

"Who are you?" came a nervous voice from within the low wooden house.

"Friends," Corum called. He said to the steersman, "Get the woman and children on board the craft." He vaulted over the rail. "We'll try to hold them off while you do that."

Jhary followed him and stood unsteadily on the ground. He was not used to a surface which did not move beneath him.

The barbarians were approaching cautiously. The leader laughed when he saw how many there were to deal with. He gave a bloodthirsty yell, cast aside his brand, drew a huge mace from his belt and spurred his pony forward, leaping the wicker barricade the farmer had erected. Corum danced aside as the mace whizzed past his helmet. He lunged. The sword caught the man in the knee and he shouted in rage. Jhary jumped through the barricade and ran to pick up the discarded brand, the other horsemen on his heels. He dashed back into the farmyard and fired the wickerwork. It began to splutter as another rider leapt his horse over it. Jhary flung his poignard and it went true to the barbarian's eye. The man screamed and fell backwards off his pony. Jhary grabbed the reins and mounted the unruly creature, yanking savagely at the bit to turn it. Meanwhile the barricade was beginning to burn and Corum dodged the mace which was studded with the fangs of animals. He saw an opening, lunged again and caught the barbarian in the side. The man went forward over his pony's neck, clutching at his wound, and was borne away across the farmyard. Corum saw others trying to force their horses to brave the smoky blaze.

Now Bwydyth was helping the farmer's young wife carry a cot to the sky ship. Two boys and an older girl came with them. The farmer, still a little dazed by what was happening, came last, holding the rusty broadsword in both hands.

Three riders leapt suddenly through the barricade and bore down on the group.

But Jhary was there. He had recovered his poignard and he flung it again. Again it went straight into the eye of the nearest rider, again the rider fell backwards, his feet easily coming free from the leather loops he used as stirrups. Corum dashed for the pony and leapt into the saddle, flinging up his sword to protect himself from a heavy war-axe aimed at him. He slid his sword down the haft of the axe and forced the man to shorten his grip on it so that it was hard to bring back. While the man struggled to raise the axe Jhary took him from the rear, stabbing him through the heart so that his sabre-point appeared on the other side of the barbarian's body. There were more barbarians now. The farmer had hacked the legs of a pony from under one and before the warrior could disentangle himself had split him from shoulder to breastbone, using the sword rather like a woodman would use an axe.

The children and the woman were on board the ship. Corum took another barbarian in the throat and leaned down to pull at the farmer who was hacking blindly at the corpse. He pointed at the ship. The farmer did not seem to understand at first, but then dropped his bloody broadsword and ran to the ship. Corum slashed at his last opponent and Jhary dismounted to recover his poignard. Corum turned the horse, extended an arm to Jhary who sheathed his weapons and took the arm, riding in the stirrup until they reached the sky ship. They both hauled themselves aboard. The ship was already rising through the smoky air. Two riders were left staring up at the disappearing ship. They did not look happy, for they had expected an easy slaying and now most of their number were dead and their prey was escaping.

"My stock," said the farmer, looking down.

"You are alive," Jhary pointed out.

Rhalina was comforting the woman. The Margravine had drawn her sword, ready to join the men if they were too hard-pressed. It lay on the seat nearby. Now she held the smallest boy in her arms and stroked his hair.

Jhary's cat peered out from a locker under the seat, was assured that the danger was over and fluttered up to settle again on its master's shoulder.

"Do you know anything of their main army?" Corum asked the farmer. The Prince in the Scarlet Robe dabbed at a minor wound he had received on his mortal hand.

"I have heard—heard things. I have heard that it is not a human army at all."

"That may be true," Corum agreed, "but do you know its whereabouts?"

"It is almost upon Halwyg—if not there already. Pray, sir, where do you take us?"

"I fear it is to Halwyg," Corum told him.

The sky ship sailed on over the desolated land. And now they could see that the bands of outriders were larger—plainly part of the main army. Many noticed the ship's passage over their heads and a few cast their lances at it or shot an arrow or two before returning to their burning, their rapine and their murder.

It was not these that Corum feared but the sorcery which Lyr-a-Brode might now command.

The farmer was peering earthwards. "Is it all like this?" he asked grimly.

"As far as we know. Two forces march on Halwyg—one from the east and one from the south-west. I doubt if the barbarians of Bro-an-Mabden are any more merciful than their comrades." Corum turned away from the rail.

"I wonder how Llarak-an-Fol fared," said Rhalina as she cradled a sleeping child. "And did Beldan stay there or was he able to continue with our men to Halwyg? And what of the duke?"

"We shall know all this soon, I hope." Jhary allowed a little dark-haired boy to stroke his cat. The cat bore the assault with gravity.

Corum moved nervously about the deck, peering ahead to seek Halwyg's beflowered towers.

Then, "There they are," said Jhary softly. "There's your host from hell."

Corum looked down and saw the tide of flesh and steel that

swept across the land. Mabden horsemen in their thousands. Mabden charioteers. Mabden infantry. And things which were not Mabden—things summoned by sorcery and recruited from the Realm of Chaos. There was the Army of the Dog—huge, loping beasts the size of horses, more vulpine than canine. There was the Army of the Bear—each massive Bear walking upright and carrying a shield and a club. And there was the Army of Chaos itself—misshapen warriors like those they had met earlier in the yellow abyss, led by a tall horseman in dazzling plate armour which clothed him from head to foot—doubtless the messenger of Queen Xiombarg of whom they had heard.

And just ahead of the host's leaders were the walls of Halwyg-nan-Vake, looking from this distance like a huge, complicated floral model.

Drums sounded from the ranks of the host of hell. Harsh trumpets cried out the Mabden bloodlust. Horrid laughter rose towards the sky ship and howls escaped the throats of the Army of the Dog—mocking howls that anticipated victory.

Corum spat down on the horde, the stench of Chaos now strong again in his nostrils. His mortal eye changed to burning black with an iris of flaming gold as his anger seized him and he spat a second time upon the flowing vileness below. He made a noise in his throat and his hand went to the hilt of his sword as he remembered all his hatred of the Mabden who had slain his family and maimed him. He saw the banner of King Lyr-a-Brode—a crude, tattered thing bearing the Sign of the Dog and the Sign of the Bear. He sought to find his great enemy, Earl Glandyth-a-Krae, amongst the ranks.

Rhalina called, "Corum—do not waste your strength now. Calm yourself and save your energy for the fight which must yet come!"

He sank down upon the seat, his mortal eye slowly fading back to its original colour. He panted like one of the Dogs that marched below and the jewels covering his faceted, alien eye seemed to shift and glitter with a different rage from his own...

Rhalina shivered when she saw him thus, with hardly any trace of the mortal about him. He was like some possessed demigod of the darkest legends of her people and her love of him turned to terror.

Corum buried his ruined head in his grafted, six-fingered hand and whimpered until the mood was driven out of him and he could look up and seem sane again. His rage and his fight to vanquish it had exhausted him. Pale and limp he lay back in the seat, one hand on the brass rail of the sky ship as it began to circle down over Halwyg.

"Not much more than a mile away," Jhary murmured. "They'll have surrounded the walls by the morning, if not stopped."

"What army of ours could stop them?" Rhalina asked him hopelessly. "Lord Arkyn's reign is to be short-lived I fear."

The drums continued to rattle out their jubilation. The trumpets continued to blare their triumph. The howls of the Army of the Dog, the grunts of the Army of the Bear, the cacklings and shriekings of the Army of Chaos, the ground-shaking thunder of the ponies' hoofs, the rumble of the iron-bound chariot wheels, the clatter of the war-gear, the creak of harness, the bellowing laughter of the barbarians, all seemed to come closer with each heartbeat as the horde of hell swept inevitably towards the City of the Flowers.

2

THE SIEGE BEGINS

THE SKY SHIP circled lower and lower over the tense and silent city as the sun began to set and the towers echoed the sounds of the satanic horde still marching relentlessly towards it.

The streets and parks of Halwyg were packed with weary soldiers, camped wherever they could find an open space. Flowers had been trampled underfoot and edible shrubs had been stripped to feed the red-eyed warriors who had been driven back to Halwyg by the barbarian force. They were so tired that only a few looked up when the sky ship passed over their heads on its way to the roof of King Onald's palace. It landed on deserted battlements but almost immediately guards, in the murex helms and the mother-o'-pearl breastplates, bearing the round shell shields of Lywm-an-Esh, with spears and swords, rushed up to apprehend them, doubtless thinking they were enemies. But when they saw Rhalina and Corum they lowered their weapons in relief. Several of them were wounded from previous encounters with the barbarian host and all looked as if they would be improved by more than a night's sleep.

"Prince Corum," said the leader, "I will tell the king that you are here."

"I thank you. In the meantime I hope some of your men will help these people here, whom we saved from Lyr's men a short time back."

"It will be done, though food is scarce."

Corum had considered this. "The sky ship here can forage for you, though it must not be endangered. It may find a little food."

The steersman took a scroll from inside his jerkin and handed it to Corum. "Here, Prince Corum, are the rare substances our city needs if it is to attempt to crash once again through the Wall Between the Realms."

"If Arkyn can be summoned," Corum told him, "I will give him this list, for he is a god and therefore more knowledgeable about such things than any of us."

In Onald's simple room, still covered with maps of his land, they found the grim-faced king.

"How fares your nation, King Onald?" Jhary-a-Conel asked him as they entered.

"It is scarcely a nation any longer. We have been forced further and further back until barely all that's left of us is gathered here in Halwyg." He pointed at a large map of Lywm-an-Esh and he spoke in a hollow voice. "The County of Arluth-a-Cal—taken by the sea-raiders from Bro-an-Mabden—the County of Pengarde and its ancient capital Enyn-an-Aldarn—burned—it flames all the way to Lake Calenyk by all reports.

I have heard that the Duchy of Oryn-nan-Calywn still resists them in its most southern mountains, as does the Duchy of Haun-a-Gwyragh—but Bedwilral-nan-Rywm is completely taken, as is the County of Gal-a-Gorow. Of the Duchy of Palantyrn-an-Kenak, I do not know..."

"Fallen," said Corum.

"Ah—fallen..."

"They close in now from all quarters it seems," Jhary said, looking carefully at the map. "They landed along each of your coasts and then systematically began to tighten their circle—the whole horde converging on Halwyg-nan-Vake. I would not have thought barbarians capable of such sophisticated tactics—or of keeping to them even if they thought of them..."

"You forget Xiombarg's messenger," Corum said. "He doubtless helped them make this plan and trained them in its manipulation."

"You speak of the creature all in brilliant armour that rides at the head of his deformed army?" King Onald said.

"Aye. What news have you of him?"

"None that can help us. He is invulnerable, by all accounts, but, as you say, has much to do with the organizing of the barbarian army. He rides often at King Lyr's side. His name, I have heard, is Gaynor—Prince Gaynor the Damned..."

Jhary nodded. "He figures often in such conflicts. He is doomed to serve Chaos through all eternity. So now he is Queen Xiombarg's lackey, is he? It is a better position than some he has attained to in the past—or the future—whichever it is..."

King Onald looked oddly at Jhary and then continued. "Even without the aid of Chaos they would outnumber us ten to one. With our better weapons and superior tactics we might have resisted them for years—at least kept them on our coasts—but this Prince Gaynor advises them on every move. And his advice is good."

"He has had plenty of experience," said Jhary, rubbing at his chin.

"How long can you withstand a siege?" Rhalina asked the king.

He shrugged and stared miserably out of the window at his crowded city. "I know not. The warriors are all weary, our walls are not particularly high, and Chaos fights on Lyr's side…"

"We had best hasten to the temple," Corum said, "and see if Lord Arkyn can be summoned."

Through the packed streets they rode, seeing hopeless faces on all sides. Carts cluttered the broad avenues and campfires burned on the lawns. Half the army seemed to bear wounds of one description or another and others were inadequately armed and armoured. It hardly seemed that Halwyg could stand Lyr's first assault. The siege would not be long, thought Corum as he tried to make faster headway through the throng.

At last they reached the temple. The grounds of this were packed with sleeping, wounded soldiers and Aleryon-a-Nyvish, the priest, was standing in the entrance to the temple as if he had known they were coming.

He welcomed them eagerly. "Did you find aid?"

"Perhaps," answered Corum. "But we must speak with Lord Arkyn. Can he be summoned?"

"He awaits you. He came not a few moments since."

They strode rapidly into the cool darkness. Mattresses filled it but they were at this time unoccupied. They awaited the wounded and the dying.

The handsome shape which Lord Arkyn had chosen to assume stepped from the shadows. "How fared you in Xiombarg's realm?"

Corum told him what had transpired and Arkyn looked disturbed by what he heard. He stretched out his hand. "Give me the scroll. I will seek the substances needed by the City in the Pyramid. But it will take even me some time to locate them."

"And in the meanwhile the fate of two besieged cities is in doubt," Rhalina said. "Gwlās-cor-Gwrys in Xiombarg's realm and Halwyg-nan-Vake here. The destiny of one depends upon the other."

"Such mirrorings are common enough in the struggle between Law and Chaos," murmured Jhary.

"Aye—they are," agreed Lord Arkyn. "But you must try to hold Halwyg until I return. Even then we cannot be sure that Gwlās-cor-Gwrys will still be standing. Our one advantage is that Queen Xiombarg now concentrates upon two battles—the one in my realm and the one in her own."

"Yet her messenger Prince Gaynor the Damned is here and seems to represent her adequately," Corum pointed out.

"If Gaynor were destroyed," Arkyn said, "much of the barbarian advantage would go. They are not natural tacticians and without him there will be some confusion."

"But their numbers alone represent a mighty big advantage," Jhary said. "And then there is the Army of the Dog and the Army of the Bear…"

"Agreed, Master Jhary. Still, I say, your most important enemy is Gaynor the Damned."

"But he is indestructible."

"He can be destroyed by one as strong and as fate-heavy as himself." Arkyn looked significantly at Corum. "But it would take much courage and could mean that both would be destroyed…"

Corum inclined his head. "I will consider what you have said, Lord Arkyn."

"And now I go."

The handsome figure vanished and they were left alone in the temple.

Corum looked at Rhalina and then he looked at Jhary. Neither met his gaze. They both knew what Lord Arkyn had asked of him—of the responsibility which had been put upon his shoulders.

He frowned, fingering the jeweled patch on his eye, flexing the fingers of the six-fingered alien hand extending from his left wrist.

"With the Eye of Rhynn and the Hand of Kwll," he said. "With Shool's obscene gifts which were grafted to my soul almost as wholly as they were grafted to my body, I will attempt to rid this realm of Prince Gaynor the Damned."

3

PRINCE GAYNOR THE DAMNED

"HE WAS ONCE a hero," said Jhary as they stood on the walls that night, peering out at the thousand campfires of the Chaos army surrounding the city, "this Prince Gaynor. He, too, fought on the side of Law. But then he fell in love with something—perhaps it was a woman—and became a renegade, throwing in his lot with Chaos. He was punished—punished, some say, by the power of the Balance. Now he may never serve Law or know the pleasure of Law. Now he must serve Chaos eternally, just as you, eternally, serve Law..."

"Eternally?" Corum said, disturbed.

"I'll speak no more of that," Jhary said. "But you sometimes know peace. Prince Gaynor only remembers peace and can never, throughout all the ages, expect to find it again."

"Not even in death?"

"He is doomed never to die, for in death there is peace, even if that death lasts only an instant before another rebirth."

"Then I cannot slay him?"

"You can slay him no more than you can slay one of the Great Old Gods. But you can banish him. You must know how to do that, however…"

"Do you know, Jhary?"

"I think so." Jhary lowered his head in concentration as he paced the walls beside Corum. "I remember tales that Gaynor can be defeated only if his visor is opened and his face looked upon by one who serves Law. But his visor can only be opened by a greater force than any mortal wields. Such is the familiar condition of a sorcerous fate. It is all I know."

"It is precious little," Corum said gracelessly.

"Aye."

"It must be tonight. They will expect no attack from us—especially on the first night of their siege. We must go against the Chaos host, strike swiftly and attempt to slay—or banish, whatever it is—Prince Gaynor the Damned. He controls the malformed army and they will be drawn back to their own realm if he is no longer present."

"A simple plan," said Jhary sardonically. "Who rides with us? Beldan is here. I have seen him."

"I'll not risk any of the defenders. They'll be needed if the plan fails. We'll ride alone," Corum said.

Jhary shrugged and sighed. "You'd best stay here, little friend," he told his cat.

Through the night they slipped, leading their horses whose hoofs were bound in thick rags to muffle their sound, towards the Camp of Chaos where the Mabden reveled and kept poor guard.

The smell was sufficient to tell them where Prince Gaynor's

hellish band was camped. The half-men shambled about in strange, ritual dances, resembling the movements of mating beasts rather than those of human folk. The stupid beast faces were slack-mouthed, dull-eyed, and they drank much sour wine to make them forget what once they had been before they had pledged themselves to the corruption that was Chaos.

Prince Gaynor sat in the middle of this, near the leaping fire, all encased from head to foot in his flashing armour. It was sometimes silver, sometimes gold, sometimes bluish steel. A dark yellow plume nodded on the helm and on the breastplate was engraved the Arms of Chaos—eight arrows radiating from a central hub, representing, according to Chaos, all the rich possibilities inherent in its philosophy. Prince Gaynor did not carouse. He did not eat and he did not drink. He merely stared at his warriors, his metal-gloved hands upon the pommel of his big sword which was also sometimes silver, sometimes gold, sometimes bluish steel. He was all of a piece, Prince Gaynor the Damned.

They had to skirt several snoring barbarian guards before they could creep into Gaynor's camp, which was set some distance from the rest of the camp, just as the Army of the Dog and the Army of the Bear were camped the other side. Some of Lyr's men staggered past them, but, because Corum and Jhary were swathed in cowled cloaks, hardly gave them a second glance. None suspected that the warriors of Lywm-an-Esh would come in couples to their camp.

When they reached the edge of the firelight and were close to the leaping throng of beast-men, they mounted their horses and waited for a long moment while they regarded the mysterious figure of Prince Gaynor the Damned.

He had not moved once since they had first observed him. Seated on an ornate, high saddle of ebony and ivory, his hands on the pommel of his great broadsword, he continued to stare without interest at the caperings of his obscene followers.

Then they rode into the circle of fiery light and Prince Corum Jhaelen Irsei, Servant of Law, faced Prince Gaynor the Damned, Servant of Chaos.

Corum wore all his Vadhagh gear—his delicate silver mail, his conical helm, his scarlet robe. His tall spear was in his right hand and his great round war-board was upon his left arm.

Prince Gaynor rose from where he was seated and lifted an arm to stop the revels. The legion of hell turned to regard Corum and they began to snarl and gibber when they recognized him.

"Be silent!" Prince Gaynor the Damned commanded, stepping forward in his flickering armour and sheathing his sword. "Saddle my charger, one of you, for I think Prince Corum and his friend come to do battle with me." His voice was vibrant and, on the surface, amused. But there was a bleak quality underlying it, a tragic sadness.

"Will you fight me alone, Prince Gaynor?" Corum asked.

The Prince of Chaos laughed. "Why should I? It is long since I subscribed to your ideas of chivalry, Prince Corum. And I have a pledge to my mistress, Queen Xiombarg, that I must use any means to destroy you. I have never known her to hate—but she hates you, Sir Vadhagh. How she hates you!"

"It could be because she fears me," Corum suggested.

"Aye. It could be."

"Then you will set your whole host upon us?"

"Why should I not? If you are foolish enough to enter my power..."

"You have no pride?"

"None, I think."

"No honour?"

"None."

"No courage?"

"I have no absolute qualities at all, I fear—save that, perhaps—save fear, itself."

"You are honest, however."

A deep laugh issued from the closed visor. "If you would believe it. Why have you come to my camp, Prince Corum?"

"You know why, do you not?"

"You hope to slay me, because I am the brain which controls all this barbarian brawn? A good idea. But I cannot be slain. Would that I could—I have prayed for death, often enough. You hope that if you defeat me you will buy time for building up your defenses. Perhaps you would do so, but I regret that I will slay you and thus rob Halwyg-nan-Vake of its chief supply of brain and resourcefulness."

"If you cannot be slain, why not fight me personally?"

"Because I would not waste time. Warriors!"

The misshapen beast-men arrayed themselves behind their master who mounted his white charger on which had been placed the high saddle of ebony and ivory. He settled his own spear in its rest and drew his own shield onto his arm.

Corum lifted his jeweled eye-patch and looked beyond Prince Gaynor and his men, into the netherworld cavern where his last victims were. Here were the Chaos pack, all the more distorted since the Ghanh had taken them into the folds of its crushing wings. There was Polib-Bav, the pack's horse-faced leader. Into the netherworld reached the Hand of Kwll and summoned the Chaos pack to Corum's aid.

"Now Chaos shall war once more with Chaos!" Corum cried. "Take your prizes, Polib-Bav, and be released from limbo!"

And foulness met foulness and horror clashed with horror as

the Chaos pack rushed into Gaynor's camp and began to set upon their brother beasts. Dog-thing fought cow-thing, horse-thing fought frog-thing, and their bludgeons and their carvers and their axes rose and fell in a frightful massing. Screams, grunts, bellows, groans, oaths, squeals, cackles rose from the heap of embattled creatures and Prince Gaynor the Damned looked at it and then turned his horse so that it faced Corum.

"I congratulate you, Prince in the Scarlet Robe. I see you did not rely upon my chivalry. Now, will both of you fight me?"

"Not that," Corum said, preparing his spear and lifting himself in his stirrups so that he was now seated on the high part of his saddle, almost standing upright. "My friend is here to report the outcome of this fight should I perish. He will only fight to protect himself."

"A fair tourney, eh?" Prince Gaynor laughed again. "Very well!" And he, too, put himself into the fighting position in his saddle.

Then he charged.

Corum spurred his own warhorse towards his foe, spear raised to strike, shield up to protect his face, for he lacked Gaynor's visor.

Prince Gaynor's flashing armour half-blinded him as he galloped on, then he flung back his arm and hurled the great spear with all his might at Gaynor's head. It struck full against the helm but did not pierce, did not appear to dent it. However, Gaynor reeled in his saddle and did not immediately retaliate with his own spear, giving Corum time to stretch out his hand and catch the haft of his weapon as it bounced back. Gaynor laughed when he saw this and jabbed at Corum's face, but the Prince in the Scarlet Robe brought up his war-board to block the blow.

Elsewhere the grisly fight between the two parties of beast-men went on. The Chaos pack was smaller than Gaynor's force, but it had the advantage that it had already been slain once and therefore could not be slain again.

Now both horses reared at once, hoofs tangling and almost throwing their riders off. Corum flung his spear as he clung to the reins. Again it struck the Prince of the Damned who was hurled backwards from his saddle and lay in the filthy mud of his camp. He sprang up at once, his spear still in his hand, and returned Corum's cast. The spear pierced the war-board and its point came a fraction of an inch to entering Corum's jeweled eye. The spear hanging in his shield, he drew his sword and charged down upon Prince Gaynor. Gaynor's helm rang with a bitter glee and now his broadsword was in his right hand, his shield raised to take Corum's first blow. Gaynor's stroke was not at Corum but at the horse. He hacked off one of its feet and it collapsed to the ground, throwing Corum sprawling.

Swiftly, in spite of his heavy plate armour, Prince Gaynor raised his sword and ran at Corum as he desperately tried to regain his footing in the mud. The sword whistled down and was met by the shield. The blade bit through the layers of leather and metal and wood but was stopped by the metal of Gaynor's own spear which was still protruding from Corum's war-board. Corum swiped at Gaynor's feet, but the Prince of the Damned leapt high and escaped the blow while Corum rolled back and at last managed to climb to a standing position, his shield all split and near useless.

Gaynor still laughed, his voice echoing in the helm that was never opened.

"You fight well, Corum, but you are mortal—and I no longer am!"

The sounds of battle had alerted the rest of the camp, but the barbarians were unsure of what was happening. They were used to obeying Lyr who had come to rely upon Gaynor's commands and now Gaynor had no time to tell Lyr what to do.

The two champions began to circle each other while to one side of them the beast-men of Chaos continued to fight to the death.

In the shadows beyond the firelight, the faces of superstitious, wide-eyed barbarians watched the fray, not understanding how this thing had come about.

Corum abandoned his shield and unslung his war-axe from his back, holding it in the six-fingered Hand of Kwll. He increased the distance between himself and his enemy, adjusting his grip on the axe. It was a perfectly balanced throwing axe, normally used by Vadhagh infantry in the old days when they had battled the Nhadragh. Corum hoped that Prince Gaynor would not realize what he intended to do.

Swiftly he raised his arm and flung the axe. It flashed through the air towards the Prince of the Damned—and was caught upon the shield.

But Gaynor staggered back under the force of the blow, his shield completely split in twain. He threw aside the pieces, took his broadsword in both hands and closed with Corum.

Corum blocked the first blow and the second and the third, being forced back by the ferocity of Gaynor's attack. He jumped to one side and aimed a darting thrust designed to pierce one of the joins in Gaynor's armour. Gaynor shifted his sword into his right hand and turned the thrust aside, taking two steps backwards. He was panting now. Corum heard his breath hissing in his helm.

"Immortal you may be, Prince Gaynor the Damned—but tireless you are not."

"You cannot slay me! Do you not think I would welcome death!"

"Then surrender to me." Corum was panting himself. His heart beat rapidly, his chest heaved. "Surrender to me and see if I cannot kill you!"

"To surrender would be to betray my pledge to Queen Xiombarg."

"So you do know honour?"

"Honour!" Gaynor laughed. "Not honour—fear, as I told you. If I betray her, Xiombarg will punish me. I do not think you could comprehend what that means, Prince in the Scarlet Robe." And again Prince Gaynor rushed upon Corum, the broadsword shrieking around his head.

Corum ducked under the whirling broadsword and came in with a swipe to Gaynor's legs so powerful that one knee buckled for an instant before the Prince of the Damned hopped backward, darting a glance over his shoulder to see how his minions fared.

The Chaos pack was finishing them. One by one the creatures Corum had summoned from the netherworld were gathering in their prizes and vanishing to whence they had come.

With a cry Gaynor threw himself once more on Corum. Corum summoned all his strength to turn the lunge and thrust back. Then Gaynor closed in, grabbing Corum's sword-arm and raising his broadsword to bring it down on Corum's head. Corum wrestled himself free and the blade struck his shoulder, cut through the first layer of mail and was stopped by the second.

And he was defenseless. Prince Gaynor had clung to his sword and now held it triumphantly in his left gauntlet.

"Yield to me, Prince Corum. Yield to me and I will spare your life."

"So that you can take me back to your mistress Xiombarg."

"It is what I must do."

"Then I will not yield!"

"So I must kill you, then?" Gaynor panted as he dropped Corum's sword to the mud, took a grip with both hands on the hilt of his own broadsword, and stumbled forward to finish his foe.

4

THE BARBARIAN ATTACK

Instinctively Corum flung up his hands to ward off Gaynor's blow and then something happened to the Hand of Kwll.

More than once the hand had saved his life—often in anticipation of the threat—and now it acted of its own volition again to reach out and grasp Gaynor's blade, wrenching it from the hands of the damned prince and bringing it rapidly up then down to dash the pommel against the top of Gaynor's head.

Prince Gaynor staggered, groaning, and slowly fell to his knees.

Now Corum jumped forward and with one arm encircled Gaynor's neck. "Do you yield, prince?"

"I cannot yield," Gaynor replied in a strangled voice. "I have nothing *to* yield."

But he no longer struggled as the sinister Hand of Kwll grasped the lip of his visor and tugged.

"NO!" Prince Gaynor cried as he realized what Corum planned. "You cannot. No mortal may see my face!" He began to writhe, but Corum held him firmly, and the Hand of Kwll tugged again at the visor.

"PLEASE!"

The visor shifted slightly.

"I BEG THEE, PRINCE IN THE SCARLET ROBE! LET ME GO AND I WILL OFFER THEE NO FURTHER HARM!"

"You have not the right to swear such an oath," Corum reminded him fiercely. "You are Xiombarg's thing and are without honour or will."

The pleading voice echoed strangely. "Have mercy, Prince Corum."

"And I have not the right to grant you that mercy, for I serve Arkyn," Corum told him.

The Hand of Kwll wrenched for a third time at the visor and it came away.

Corum stared at a youthful face which writhed as if composed of a million white worms. Dead, red eyes peered from the face and all the horrors Corum had ever witnessed could not compare with the simple, tragic horror of that visage. He screamed and his scream blended with that of Prince Gaynor the Damned as the flesh of the face began to putrefy and change into a score of foul colours which gave off a more pungent stench than anything which had issued from the Chaos pack itself. And as Corum watched the face changed its features. Sometimes it was the face of a middle-aged man, sometimes the face of a woman, sometimes that of a boy—and once, fleetingly, he recognized his own face. How many guises had Prince Gaynor known through all the eternity of his damnation? Corum saw a million years of despair recorded there. And still the face writhed, still the red eyes blazed in terror and agony, still the features changed and changed and changed and changed…

More than a million years. Aeons of misery. The price of Gaynor's nameless crime, his betrayal of his oath to Law. A fate imposed upon him not by Law but by the power of the Balance. What crime could it have been if the neutral Cosmic Balance had been required to act? Some suggestion of it appeared and disappeared in the various features that flashed within the helm. And now Corum did not grip Gaynor's neck, but instead cradled the tormented head in his arms and wept for the Prince of the Damned who had paid a price—was paying a price—which no being should ever have to pay.

Here, Corum felt as he wept, was the ultimate in justice—or the ultimate in injustice. Both seemed at that moment to be the same.

And even now Prince Gaynor was not dying. He was merely undergoing a transition from one existence to another. Soon, in some other distant realm, far from the Fifteen Planes and the realms of the Sword Rulers, he would be doomed to continue his servitude to Chaos.

At last the face disappeared and the flashing armour was empty.

Prince Gaynor the Damned was gone.

Corum lifted his head dazedly and heard Jhary-a-Conel's voice in his ears. "Quickly, Corum, take Gaynor's horse. The barbarians are gathering their courage. Our work is done here!"

The companion to champions was shaking him. Corum got up, found his sword where Gaynor had dropped it in the mud, let Jhary help him into the ebony-and-ivory saddle…

…Then they were galloping towards the walls of Halwyg-nan-Vake with the Mabden warriors howling behind them.

The gates opened for them and closed instantly. Barbarian fists beat uselessly on the iron-shod timbers as they dismounted to find that King Onald and Rhalina were waiting for them.

"Prince Gaynor?" said King Onald eagerly. "Does he still live?"

"Aye," Corum answered hollowly. "He still lives."

"Then you failed!"

"No." Corum walked away from them, leading his foe's horse, walking into the darkness, unwilling to speak to anyone, not even Rhalina.

King Onald followed him and then paused, looking up at Jhary who was lowering himself from his saddle. "He did not fail?"

"Prince Gaynor's power is gone," Jhary said tiredly. "Corum defeated him. Now the barbarians have no brain—they have only their numbers, their brutality, their Dogs and their Bears." He laughed without humour. "That is all, King Onald."

They all stared after Corum who, with bowed back and dragging feet, passed into the shadows.

"I will prepare us for their attack," Onald said. "They will come at us in the morning, I think."

"It is likely," Rhalina agreed. She had an impulse to go to Corum then, but she restrained it.

And at dawn the barbarian army of King Lyr-a-Brode joined with the army of Bro-an-Mabden and, still with the strength of the Army of the Dog and the Army of the Bear, began to close in on Halwyg-nan-Vake.

Warriors were packed on all Halwyg's low walls. The barbarians had no siege engines with them, since they had relied on Prince Gaynor's strategy and his host of Chaos in their taking of all other cities. But there were many of them—so many that it was almost impossible to see the last ranks of their legions. They rode on horses and in chariots or they marched.

Corum had rested for a few hours but had not been able to sleep. He could not rid himself of the vision of Prince Gaynor's face. He tried to remember his hatred of Glandyth-a-Krae and sought the earl amongst the barbarian horde, but Glandyth was apparently nowhere present. Perhaps he searched for Corum still in the region of Moidel's Mount?

King Lyr sat on a big horse and clutched his own crude battle-banner. Beside him was the humpbacked shape of King Cronekyn-a-Drok, ruler of the tribes of Bro-an-Mabden. Half-idiot was King Cronekyn and well was he nicknamed the Little Toad.

The barbarians marched raggedly, without much order and it seemed that the sunken-featured king looked about him nervously as if he were not sure he could control such a force now that Prince Gaynor was gone.

King Lyr-a-Brode lifted his great iron sword and a sheet of flaming arrows suddenly leapt from behind his horsemen and whistled over the walls of Halwyg, setting light to shrubs which had dried from lack of watering. But King Onald had prepared for this and for some days the citizens had been preserving their urine to throw upon the flames. King Onald had heard of the fate of other besieged cities in his kingdom and he had learned what was necessary.

Several of the defenders staggered about on the walls beating at the flaming arrows which stuck in them. One man ran by Corum with his face burning but Corum hardly noticed him.

With a huge roar the barbarians rode right up to the walls and began to scale them.

The attack on Halwyg had begun in earnest.

But Corum watched for the Army of the Dog and the Army of the Bear, wondering when they would be brought against them. They seemed to be holding them in reserve and he could not quite see why.

Now his attention was forced back to the immediate threat as a gasping barbarian, brand in one hand, sword in his teeth, hauled himself over the battlements. He gave a yell of surprise as Corum cut him down. But others were coming now.

All through that morning Corum fought mechanically, though he fought well. Elsewhere on the walls Rhalina, Jhary and Beldan were commanding detachments of defenders. A thousand barbarians died, but a thousand more replaced them, for Lyr had had the sense at least to rest his men and bring them up in waves. There was no chance of such strategy amongst those who manned the walls. Every warrior who could carry a sword was being used.

Corum's ears rang with the roar and the clash of battle. He must have taken a score of lives, yet he was hardly aware of it. His mail was torn in a dozen places, he was bleeding from several minor wounds, but he did not notice that, either.

More flame arrows crossed the walls and the women and children came with buckets to douse the fires that started.

Behind the defenders was a thin haze of smoke. Before them was a mass of stinking barbarian warriors. And everywhere was the hysteria of battle. Blood splashed all surfaces. Human guts smeared the walls. Broken weapons littered the ground and corpses were piled several deep on the battlements in a vain attempt to raise the walls and stem the attack.

Below them, at the gates, barbarians used tree trunks to try to split the iron-shod wood, but so far they had held.

Corum, only distantly aware of the noise and the sights

of battle, knew that his fight with Prince Gaynor had been worthwhile. There was no doubt that Gaynor's hell-creatures and Gaynor's tactics would have taken the city by now.

But how much time was there? When would Arkyn return with the substances needed by Prince Yurette? And did the City in the Pyramid still stand?

Corum smiled grimly then. Xiombarg would know by now that he had slain her servant, Prince Gaynor. Her anger would be that much greater, her sense of impotence the stronger. Perhaps this would lessen the fury of her attack upon Gwlãs-cor-Gwrys?

Or perhaps it would strengthen it?

Corum strove to banish the speculations from his mind. There was no use in them. He picked up a spear, hurled by a barbarian, and flung it back so that it pierced the stomach of a Mabden attacker who clutched the shaft and swayed on the wall for a moment before toppling head over heels to join the other corpses on the ground below.

Then, soon after noon, the barbarians began to retreat, dragging their dead with them.

Corum saw King Lyr and King Cronekyn conferring. Perhaps they were wondering whether to bring up the Army of the Dog and the Army of the Bear. Were they considering new strategy which would not waste so many of their men? Perhaps they did not care about the men they wasted?

A boy found Corum on the wall. "Prince Corum, a message. Will you join Aleryon at the temple?"

On aching legs Corum left the battlements and got into a chariot, driving it slowly through the streets to the temple.

And now the temple was packed with wounded both within and without. Corum met Aleryon at the entrance.

"Is Arkyn returned?"

"He is, prince."

Corum strode in, looking questioningly at the prone bodies on the floor.

"They are dying," said Aleryon quietly. "They are hardly aware of anything. There is no need for discretion with these poor lads."

Arkyn stepped again from the shadows. For all he was a god and the form he assumed was not his true form, he looked tired. "Here," he said, handing Corum a small box of plain, dull metal. "Do not open it for the substances are very powerful and their radiance can kill you. Take it to the messenger from Gwlās-cor-Gwrys and tell him to go back through the Wall Between the Realms in his sky ship…"

"But he has not the power to return?" Corum argued.

"I will manufacture an opening for him—or at least I hope I will, for I am close to exhaustion. Xiombarg is working against me in subtle ways. I am not sure I will be able to find an opening near to his city, but I will try. If it is far from his city he may be in danger trying to get back there, but it will be the best I can do."

Corum nodded and took the box. "Let us pray that Gwlās-cor-Gwrys still stands."

Arkyn gave a sardonic smile. "Do not pray to me, then," he said. "For I know no better than you."

Corum hurried from the temple with the box under his arm. It was heavy and it throbbed. He climbed into his chariot, whipped up the horses and raced through the miserable avenues until he came at last to King Onald's palace. Up the steps he rushed until he came to the roof where the sky ship awaited him. He handed the box to the steersman and told him what Lord Arkyn had said. The steersman looked dubious but took the box and placed it carefully in a locker in the wheelhouse.

"Farewell, Bwydyth-a-Horn," Corum said earnestly. "May you

find your City in the Pyramid and may you bring it back to this realm in time."

Bwydyth saluted him as he took the ship into the air. Suddenly a ragged gap appeared in the sky. It was unstable. It quivered and it sparked. Beyond it a vivid golden sky could be seen, scarred with purple and orange light which shouted.

Through the gap went the sky ship. It was swallowed suddenly and the gap shrank behind it until there was no gap there at all.

Corum stood watching the sky for a moment before he heard a great roar suddenly go up from the walls.

A new attack must be beginning.

He ran down the steps, back through the palace, out into the street. And then he saw the women. They were on their knees. They were weeping. A board was being borne on the shoulders of four tall warriors. On the board was something covered by a cloak.

"What is it?" Corum asked one of the warriors. "Who is dead?"

"They have slain our King Onald," said the warrior sorrowfully. "And they have sent the Armies of the Dog and the Horned Bear against us. Destruction comes to Halwyg, Prince Corum. Now nothing can stop it!"

5

THE FURY OF QUEEN XIOMBARG

SAVAGELY CORUM WHIPPED the horses back through the streets to the wall. A silence had fallen upon the citizens of Halwyg-nan-Vake and now, it seemed, they waited passively for the death which the victorious barbarians would bring them. Already two women had committed suicide as he passed, hurling themselves from the roofs of their houses. Perhaps they were wise, he thought.

He jumped from the chariot and ran up the steps to the wall where Rhalina and Jhary-a-Conel stood together. He did not need to listen to what they told him, for he could see what was coming.

The great Dogs, eyes glaring, tongues lolling, were loping swiftly towards the city, towering over the barbarians who ran beside them. And behind the Dogs came the gigantic Bears with their clubs and their shields and with black horns curling from their heads, lumbering on their hind legs.

Corum knew that the Dogs could leap the walls and that

the Bears would batter down the gates with their clubs and he reached a decision.

"To the palace!" he shouted. "All warriors to the palace. All civilians find what cover they can!"

"You are abandoning the citizens?" Rhalina asked him, shivering when she saw that his single eye burned black and gold.

"I am doing what I can for them, hoping that our retreat will bring us a little time. From the palace we shall be able to defend ourselves better. Hurry!" he shouted. "Hurry!"

Some of the warriors moved swiftly, in relief, but others were reluctant.

Corum stayed on the walls, watching as the soldiers straggled back towards the distant palace, herding the citizens with them, carrying the wounded.

Soon only he, Rhalina and Jhary remained on the walls, watching the Dogs lope nearer, watching the Bears come closer.

Then the three companions descended to the streets and began to run through the ruined, deserted avenues, past burned bushes and crushed flowers and corpses, until they arrived at the palace and supervised the barricading of windows and doors.

The howls of the Dogs and the Bears, the yells of the triumphant barbarians could now be heard in the distance.

A kind of peace fell over the waiting palace as the three companions climbed to the roof and stood watching.

"How long?" Rhalina whispered. "How long, Corum, before they come?"

"The beasts? Some minutes before they reach the walls."

"And then?"

"A few more minutes while they nose about for a trap."

"And then?"

"A minute or two before they attack the palace. And then—I do not know. We cannot stand for long against such powerful foes."

"Have you no other plan?"

"I have one more plan. But against so many..." His voice trailed off. "I am not sure. I simply do not know the power..."

The howling and grunting grew louder, then stopped.

"They are at the walls," said Jhary.

Corum arranged his torn, scarlet robe about his shoulders. He kissed Rhalina. "Farewell, my Margravine," he said.

"Farewell? What—?"

"Farewell, Jhary—Companion to Champions. I think you may have to find another hero to befriend."

Jhary tried to smile. "Do you want me with you?"

"No."

The first of the huge Dogs leapt the wall and stood panting in the street, sniffing this way and that. They saw it in the distance.

Corum left them as they watched, going back down the steps within the palace, squeezing through the barricade at the entrance and walking out down the broad path, past the gates of the palace, until he stood in the main avenue looking towards the walls.

Some bushes were burning nearby. Gardens and lawns were littered with the dead and the near-dead. A small, winged cat circled over Corum's head and then flew back towards the battlements.

More Dogs had leapt the walls and, heads down, tongues panting, eyes wary, came slowly along the avenue to where the single small figure of Corum waited for them.

Behind the Dogs the main gates of the city suddenly splintered, cracked and were forced down. The first of the Horned Bears waddled through, nostrils dilating, club ready.

Corum was seen to raise his hand to his jeweled eye then. He was seen to blanch and stagger slightly, he was seen to stretch out his sorcerous Hand of Kwll and it vanished so that it seemed he had only a stump on his wrist.

And then, all around him, frightful things suddenly appeared. Ghastly, ruined, misshapen things—the things which had been the followers of Prince Gaynor the Damned and were now loyal to Corum only because he promised them release if they would find new victims to imprison in the Cavern of Limbo.

Corum pointed with the Hand of Kwll which had now reappeared.

Rhalina turned her horrified gaze to Jhary-a-Conel who viewed the scene with a certain equanimity. "How can such— such maimed things hope to beat those Dogs and those Bears and the thousands of barbarians who follow behind them?"

Jhary said, "I do not know. I think Corum is testing their power. If they are beaten completely, then it means that the Hand of Kwll and the Eye of Rhynn are all but useless to him and will not be able to save us if we try to escape."

"And that is what he knew and did not speak of," said Rhalina, nodding her beautiful head.

The creatures of Chaos began to race up the avenue towards the gigantic Dogs and Bears. The animals were puzzled, growling a little, but not sure whether these were friends or foes.

Scampering, malformed things they were, many with limbs missing, many with huge gaping wounds, some with no heads, some with no legs at all, so that they clung to their fellows or, where they could, propelled themselves on their hands. A wretched mob with but one advantage—they were already dead.

Down the long, desolated avenue they poured and the Dogs barked, their voices reverberating among the roofs of ruined Halwyg, warning the creatures to go back.

But the creatures came on. They could not stop. To slay the

Army of the Dog and the Army of the Bear was to assure their release from terrifying limbo—to assure that their souls might die completely—and true death was all they sought now.

Corum remained where he was at the end of the avenue and he could not believe that such wounded creatures could possibly overcome the fierce and agile beasts. He saw that all the Bears had entered the gates and that the barbarians were crowding in behind them, led by King Lyr and King Cronekyn. He hoped that even if the Chaos things were not successful a part of an hour might be granted Halwyg before the attack on the palace began.

He looked back, behind the palace, to where the roof of the Temple of Law could just be seen. Was Arkyn there? Was Arkyn waiting to see what would happen?

The Dogs began to snap at the first of the Chaos creatures to reach them. One of the huge beasts flung its head back with an armless, struggling living-dead thing in its jaws. It shook it and flung it aside, but it began to crawl towards the Dog again, the moment it had fallen. The Dog flattened its ears and its tail drooped when it saw this.

Large as they were, thought Corum, fierce as they were, they were still dogs. It was one of the things he had counted upon.

The Bears moved forward, red mouths glistening with white fangs, clubs and shields raised, striking about them with their bludgeons so that Chaos creatures were flung in all directions. But they did not die. They picked themselves up and they attacked again.

Chaos creatures clung to the fur of the Dogs and the Bears. One Dog went down at last, threshing on its back as Corum's maimed corpses tore out its throat. Corum smiled an unpleasant smile.

But now he saw that what he feared might happen was happening. Lyr-a-Brode was leading his riders around the fighting beasts. They moved warily, but they were beginning to fill the approach to the long avenue.

Corum turned and ran back towards the palace.

Before he had reached the roof the barbarians were pouring down the avenue towards the palace, while behind them the Army of the Dog and the Army of the Bear still struggled with the living-dead Chaos creatures.

Arrows whirred from the windows of the palace and Corum saw that King Cronekyn was one of the first to fall with an arrow in each eye. King Lyr-a-Brode was better armoured than his brother monarch and the arrows merely bounced off his helmet and breastplate. He waved his sword in mockery of the archers and flung his barbarians against the palace. They began to batter down the barricades.

A captain of the Royal Guard came running to the roof. "We can hold the lower floors a few moments longer, Prince Corum, but that is all."

Corum nodded. "Retreat as slowly as you can. We'll join you soon."

Rhalina said, "What did you think would happen down there, Corum?"

"I have a feeling that Xiombarg is exerting great pressures on this realm since I destroyed Prince Gaynor. I thought she might have the power to turn those things upon me."

"But she cannot personally come to this realm," Rhalina said. "We were told that. It would be to sin against the Rule of the

Balance and even the Great Old Gods will not defy the Cosmic Balance so openly."

"Perhaps," said Corum. "But I am beginning to suspect that Xiombarg's fury is so great she may attempt to break through into this realm."

"That will mean the end of us without doubt," she murmured. "What is Arkyn doing?"

"Engaging himself with what he can. He cannot interfere directly in our aid—and I suspect that he, too, prepares himself for Xiombarg. Come, we had best join the defenders."

They were two flights down when they saw the retreating warriors vainly trying to force back the roaring barbarians who pressed blindly upwards, careless of the threat of death. The captain who had earlier addressed Corum spread his hands hopelessly. "There are more detachments elsewhere in the palace, but I fear they're as hard-pressed as we."

Corum looked at the steps which were crowded with the invaders. The wall of guards was thin and would soon break. "Then we must go to the roof," he said. "At least we will be able to hold them there a little longer. We must conserve our forces as best we can."

"But we are defeated are we not, Prince Corum?" said the captain calmly.

"I fear so, captain. I fear so."

And then, from somewhere, they heard a scream. It was not a human scream and yet it was plainly a scream of pure anger.

Rhalina covered her face with her hands. "Xiombarg?" she whispered. "It is Xiombarg's voice, Corum."

Corum's mouth was dry. He could not answer her. He licked his lips.

The scream came again. But there was another sound with

it—a humming which rose higher and higher in pitch until it hurt their ears.

"The roof!" Corum cried. "Quickly."

Gasping for breath they reached the roof and flung up their arms to protect their eyes against the powerful lights which swam in the sky and obscured the sun.

Corum saw it first. Xiombarg's face, contorted with insensate fury, huge upon the horizon, her auburn hair flowing as clouds might flow across the sky, a mighty sword in her hand, large enough to slice the whole world in twain.

"It is she," groaned Rhalina. "The Queen of the Swords. She has defied the Balance and she has come to destroy us."

"Look there!" Jhary-a-Conel cried. "That is why she is here. She has followed them to our realm! They have escaped her. All her plans were thwarted and she defied the Balance in her impotence and her rage!"

It was the City in the Pyramid. It hovered in the sky over battered Halwyg-nan-Vake, its green light flickering and threatening to fade and then bursting into increased brilliance. From the City in the Pyramid came the whining sound they had heard.

Something left the city and flew down towards the palace. Corum turned away from the image of Xiombarg's raging face and her waving sword and he watched the sky ship descend. In it was the King Without a Country. He held something in his arms.

The sky ship settled on the roof and the King Without a Country smiled at Corum. "A gift," he said. "In return for your help to Gwlās-cor-Gwrys..."

"I thank you," Corum said, "but this is no time—"

"The gift has powers. It is a weapon. Take it."

Corum took the thing. It was a cylinder covered in peculiar designs and with a spade-grip at one end. The other end tapered.

"It is a weapon," repeated Noreg-Dan. "It will destroy those at whom you point it."

Corum looked at the vision of Xiombarg, heard her screaming begin again, saw her raise the sword. He pointed it at her.

"No," said the King Without a Country. "Not Xiombarg for she is a Great Old God—a Sword Ruler. Your mortal enemies."

Corum rushed to the stairs and descended. The barbarians, King Lyr now leading them, had reached the last flight.

"Point it and press the handle," called Noreg-Dan.

Corum pointed at King Lyr-a-Brode. The tall king was striding up the stairs, his braided beard fluttering, his bearing triumphant and all his huge Grim Guard behind him. He saw Corum and he laughed.

"Do you wish to surrender, last of the Vadhagh?"

And Corum laughed back at him. "I am not the last of the Vadhagh, King Lyr-a-Brode, as this shows you." He pressed the grip and suddenly the king clutched at his chest, choked and fell backwards into the arms of his Guard, his tongue protruding from his lips, his grey braids falling over his eyes.

"He is dead!" shrieked the leader of the Grim Guard. "Our king! Vengeance!"

Waving his sword he rushed at Corum. But again Corum depressed the grip and he, too, died in the manner of his king. Corum pointed the weapon several times. Each time a Grim Guard fell until there were no more Grim Guards living.

He looked back at the King Without a Country. Noreg-Dan was smiling. "We used such things against Xiombarg's minions. That is one of the reasons why she expresses such rage. It will take her time to create new mortal things to do her work."

"But she has defied the Balance in one respect," Corum said. "She may defy it in another."

The monstrous, beautiful, furious face of the Queen of the Swords rose higher over the horizon and now her shoulders could be seen, her breasts, her waist.

"AH! CORUM! DREADFUL ASSASSIN OF ALL I LOVE!"

The voice was so loud that it made Corum's ears throb with pain. He staggered backwards against the battlements, watching, transfixed, as the great sword filled the sky and Xiombarg's eyes blazed like two mighty suns. She was engulfing the world with her presence. The sword began to fall and Corum readied himself for death. Rhalina rushed to his arms and they hugged one another.

Then: "YOU HAVE MOCKED THE RULING OF THE COSMIC BALANCE, SISTER XIOMBARG!"

Against the far horizon stood Arkyn, as gigantic as the Queen of the Swords. Lord Arkyn of Law in all his godly finery, with a sword in his hand as large as Xiombarg's. And the city and its inhabitants were more insignificant than a tiny ant-nest and its occupants would be to two humans confronting each other in a meadow.

"YOU HAVE MOCKED THE BALANCE, QUEEN OF THE SWORDS."

"I AM NOT THE FIRST!"

"THERE IS ONLY ONE WHO HAS SURVIVED AND HE IS THE NAMELESS FORCE! YOU HAVE RELINQUISHED YOUR RIGHT TO RULE YOUR REALM!"

"NO! THE BALANCE HAS NO POWER OVER ME!"

"BUT IT HAS..."

And the Cosmic Balance, that Corum had seen once before in a vision after he had banished Arioch of Chaos, appeared in the sky between Lord Arkyn and Queen Xiombarg, and it was so great that it dwarfed them.

"IT HAS,"

said a voice that was not the voice of Xiombarg or Arkyn.
And the Balance began to tip towards Arkyn.

"IT HAS."

Queen Xiombarg screamed in fear and it was a scream that
shook the whole world and threatened to send it spinning from
its course about the sun.

"IT HAS."

The sword that was the symbol of her power was wrenched
effortlessly from her hand and appeared for an instant in the
bowl of the Balance which tilted towards Lord Arkyn.

"NO!" begged Queen Xiombarg. "IT WAS A TRICK—ARKYN
PLANNED THIS. HE LURED ME HERE. HE KNEW..." Her
voice was fading. "*He knew... He knew...*"

And the substance of Queen Xiombarg began to disperse. It
drifted away like wisps of cloud and then was gone.

For a moment the Cosmic Balance remained framed in the
sky, then that, too, disappeared.

Only Lord Arkyn remained now, all clothed in white radiance,
his white sword in his hand.

"IT IS DONE!" said his voice and it seemed that warmth
flooded through all the world.

"IT IS DONE!"

Corum cried, "Lord Arkyn! Did you know that Xiombarg's
fury would be so great that she would risk the wrath of the
Balance and enter this realm."

"I HOPED IT. I MERELY HOPED IT."

"Then much of what you have asked me to do was with this in mind?"

"AYE."

Corum thought of all the bitterness he had experienced, all the strife. He thought of Prince Gaynor's thousands of faces flickering before him...

"I could come to hate all gods," he said.

"IT WOULD BE YOUR RIGHT. WE MUST USE MORTALS FOR ENDS WE CANNOT OURSELVES ACHIEVE."

And then Lord Arkyn had vanished also and all that was left were the circling sky ships of Gwlās-cor-Gwrys sending down invisible death to the shrieking, terrified barbarians who were scattering now all over the churned lawns, avenues and gardens of Halwyg-nan-Vake.

Beyond the walls a few barbarians were fleeing, but the sky ships found them. The sky ships found them all.

Corum noted that the Army of the Dog and the Army of the Bear had gone, as had the creatures of Chaos he had summoned to his aid. Had they been recalled by their masters—the Dog and the Horned Bear—or were they now occupying the Cavern of Limbo. He put a finger to his jeweled eye-patch but then dropped it. He could not bear, for a long time, to look upon that netherworld.

The King Without a Country came forward. "You see how useful the gift was, Prince Corum."

"Aye."

"And now Xiombarg is banished from her realm only one more realm has a Sword Ruler. Mabelode must fear us now."

"I am sure that he does," said Corum without joy.

"And I am no longer a king without a country. I can begin to rebuild my kingdom once I have returned to my own plane."

"That is good," said Corum tonelessly.

He went to the battlements and he looked down at the corpse-strewn city. A few of the citizens were beginning to emerge from their houses. The power of the Mabden barbarians was ended for ever. Peace had come to Arkyn's realm and peace, no doubt, would come to the realm now to be ruled by his brother Lord of Law.

"Shall we return to Moidel in the sea?" Rhalina asked him softly, stroking his haggard face.

He shrugged. "I doubt if it exists. Glandyth would have razed it."

"And what of Earl Glandyth?" Jhary-a-Conel stroked the chin of his purring, winged cat which sat again upon his shoulder. "Where is he? What became of him?"

"I do not think he is dead," said Corum. "I think I shall encounter him again. I have served Law and performed all the deeds Arkyn asked of me. But I have still to take my vengeance."

A sky ship came towards them. In its prow stood the old, handsome Vadhagh Prince Yurette. He was smiling as the ship of the air settled on the roof. "Corum. Will you guest with us at Gwlās-cor-Gwrys? I wish to speak on matters concerning the restoration of Vadhagh lands, of Vadhagh castles—so that your land may once again be called Bro-an-Vadhagh. We will send the remaining Mabden back to their original kingdom of Bro-an-Mabden and the pleasant forests and fields will bloom again."

And at last Corum's gaunt face softened and he smiled.

"I thank you, Prince Yurette. We should be honoured to guest with you."

"Now that we have returned to our own realm, I think we shall cease our venturings for a while," said Prince Yurette.

"And," Corum added feelingly, "I hope that I, too, may cease my own venturings. A little tranquility would be welcome."

Far out across the plain the City in the Pyramid was beginning to descend to Earth.

EPILOGUE

GLANDYTH-A-KRAE WAS WEARY, as were his men, the charioteers who massed behind him. From the cover of the hill he had witnessed the confrontation between Queen Xiombarg and Lord Arkyn and he had seen his folk destroyed by the Vadhagh Shefanhow in their sorcerous flying craft.

For many months he had sought Corum Jhaelen Irsei and that *gast* of a renegade, the Margravine Rhalina. And at last he had turned from his search to join the main army in its attack upon Halwyg-nan-Vake, only to witness the sudden defeat of the Mabden horde and its allies.

Earl Glandyth glowered. It was he who was the outlaw now—he who must hide and scheme and know fear—for the Vadhagh had returned and Law ruled all.

At last, as night fell, and the world was illuminated by the strange green glow from the monstrous, sorcerous city, Glandyth ordered his men to go back along the road they had travelled, back to the sea and into the dark forests of the north-east. And he vowed he would yet find an ally strong enough to destroy Corum and all that Corum loved.

And he believed he knew whom to summon.

He believed he knew.

THIS ENDS
THE SECOND BOOK OF CORUM

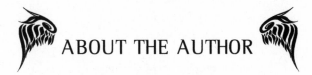

ABOUT THE AUTHOR

ORN IN LONDON in 1939, Michael Moorcock now lives in Texas. A prolific and award-winning writer with more than eighty works of fiction and non-fiction to his name, he is the creator of Elric, Jerry Cornelius and Colonel Pyat, amongst many other memorable characters. In 2008, *The Times* named Moorcock in their list of "The 50 greatest British writers since 1945".

ALSO AVAILABLE FROM
TITAN BOOKS AND TITAN COMICS

A NOMAD OF THE TIME STREAMS
The Warlord of the Air
The Land Leviathan
The Steel Tsar

THE ETERNAL CHAMPION SERIES
The Eternal Champion
Phoenix in Obsidian
The Dragon in the Sword

THE CORUM SERIES
The Knight of the Swords
The King of the Swords (July 2015)
The Bull and the Spear (August 2015)
The Oak and the Ram (September 2015)
The Sword and the Stallion (October 2015)

THE CORNELIUS QUARTET
The Final Programme (February 2016)
A Cure for Cancer (March 2016)
The English Assassin (April 2016)
The Condition of Muzak (May 2016)

THE MICHAEL MOORCOCK LIBRARY
Elric of Melniboné
Elric: Sailor on the Seas of Fate (June 2015)

MICHAEL MOORCOCK'S ELRIC
Volume 1: The Ruby Throne
Volume 2: Stormbringer

Gloucester Library
P.O. Box 2380
Gloucester, VA 23061